Henry T. Stanton

The Moneyless Man and Other Poems

Second Edition

Henry T. Stanton

The Moneyless Man and Other Poems
Second Edition

ISBN/EAN: 9783744711678

Printed in Europe, USA, Canada, Australia, Japan

Cover: Foto ©Andreas Hilbeck / pixelio.de

More available books at **www.hansebooks.com**

THE MONEYLESS MAN

AND OTHER POEMS

BY

HENRY T STANTON

[SECOND EDITION]

CINCINNATI
ROBERT CLARKE & CO
1884

PREFACE.

The exhaustion of a first edition of this volume, and the continuance of a steady demand for it, has induced the preparation of this new and revised edition. The size of the work has been increased by the addition of many new poems, and the author now presents the book to his friends and the poetry-loving public with confidence, and trusts it may meet the same generous welcome which has heretofore been bestowed upon his literary efforts.

H. T. S.

THE MONEYLESS MAN

AND OTHER POEMS

CONTENTS.

THE MONEYLESS MAN.

Is there no secret place on the face of the earth,
Where charity dwelleth, where virtue has birth?
Where bosoms in mercy and kindness will heave,
When the poor and the wretched shall ask and
    receive?
Is there no place at all, where a knock from the
    poor,
Will bring a kind angel to open the door?
Ah, search the wide world wherever you can
There is no open door for a Moneyless Man!

Go, look in yon hall where the chandelier's light
Drives off with its splendor the darkness of night,
Where the rich-hanging velvet in shadowy fold
Sweeps gracefully down with its trimmings of gold,
And the mirrors of silver take up, and renew,
In long lighted vistas the 'wildering view:
Go there! at the banquet, and find, if you can,
A welcoming smile for a Moneyless Man!

9

Go, look in yon church of the cloud-reaching spire,
Which gives to the sun his same look of red fire,
Where the arches and columns are gorgeous within,
And the walls seem as pure as a soul without sin ;
Walk down the long aisles, see the rich and the great
In the pomp and the pride of their worldly estate ;
Walk down in your patches, and find, if you can,
Who opens a pew to a Moneyless Man.

Go, look in the Banks, where Mammon has told
His hundreds and thousands of silver and gold ;
Where, safe from the hands of the starving and poor,
Lies pile upon pile of the glittering ore !
Walk up to their counters — ah, there you may stay
'Til your limbs grow old, 'til your hairs grow gray,
And you 'll find at the Banks not one of the clan
With money to lend to a Moneyless Man !

Go, look to yon Judge, in his dark-flowing gown,
With the scales wherein law weigheth equity down ;
Where he frowns on the weak and smiles on the
          strong,
And punishes right whilst he justifies wrong ;
Where juries their lips to the Bible have laid,
To render a verdict — they 've already made :
Go there, in the court-room, and find, if you can,
Any law for the cause of a Moneyless Man !

Then go to your hovel — no raven has fed
The wife who has suffered too long for her bread ;

Kneel down by her pallet, and kiss the death-frost
From the lips of the angel your poverty lost:
Then turn in your agony upward to God,
And bless, while it smites you, the chastening rod,
And you 'll find, at the end of your life's little span,
There 's a welcome above for a Moneyless Man!

NAMELESS.

THERE were great lights from the palace
　　Streaming on the outer trees,
That, with fleckings thro' the trellis,
　　Played a-tremor at his knees,
As a minstrel stranger, friendless,
　　Underneath the walls of Fame
Sat in silence, whilst the endless
　　Notes of glory-music came.

Paths, to him, were bleak and aimless,
　　As he sat within the shade,
Telling o'er the wonders, nameless,
　　That his poet-heart had made:
"Could he pass the amber portal,
　　And the jasper halls along,
Where the poet-souls immortal
　　Held their revelry of song?

"Could he strike a chord of sorrow
　　In the upper, choral spheres,
Where to-morrow, and to-morrow,
　　It would echo down the years?

Could he grasp the ivy clinging
   At the marble casement, now,
And amid the spirits singing,
   Wear it, deathless, on his brow?"

Once he thought to climb the terrace
   To the open, opal gate,
Where, beyond the sweeping arras,
   Swelled the voices of the great;
Where the stricken harp-strings golden
   Gave their notes in high accord
To the music-stories olden,
   To the glory of the LORD.

But his soul, untaught and simple,
   Shrinking outward, turned away,
Where the great lights from the temple
   Drove the night-time from the day:
" I shall seek the shadow, yonder
   Underneath the silent pine ;
There are harp-notes higher, grander
   Than may ever be from mine ! "

Soft he touched the strings, like Summer
   Touching o'er the barren trees,
And the night bore out their murmur,
   Through its alleys, to the seas ;
Softer, sweeter went the cadence
   Through the branches and above,

B

As come visions unto maidens
 In the budding-time of love.

Through the gates of opal splendor,
 And along the jasper wall,
Pass the notes of music tender,
 Through the corridor and hall;
And his tones sweep in the chamber
 From the shadow and the gloom,
And their liquid echoes clamber
 Up the arras to the dome.

And they rise and fall like billows,
 In the alcoves of the air,
Passing in and out the willows,
 And across beyond the mere;
High, and grand, and godly power
 Sweeps along the palace caves,
'Til the ivy-vine, in flower,
 Trembles music from its leaves.

And the poet-souls may listen
 To the outer harp to-night,
And the great lamps gleam and glisten
 In an ecstacy of light;
These are music-tones undying,
 These are worthy highest name,
From the poet-spirit lying
 Underneath the walls of Fame.

CASTE.

If, as a burn,
That from the shadow fleeing,
Seeks the shine
On some broad river,
I now could turn
The current of my being
Into thine,
To flow forever —
Believest thou this tribute-blood
Would give thy veins to darker flood?

The tuneful brooks
That down the slopes are going
To the sea
With music-laughter,
In hidden nooks
Begin their silver flowing,
Silently,
To chorus after.
Believest thou, because obscure
Of origin, they are not pure?

Not in the grand,
Resistless, moving river,
Do we find
The lucent crystal;
But out the land
The springs run limpid ever,
Overtwined
By vine and thistle :
Not from the pure, pearled fountain veins
Do rivers take their *débris* stains.

O, maid !   O, queen !
O, proud and pulsing woman !
· If the tide
That floods these valleys,
Less pure were seen
Than that in any human,
It should hide
In covert alleys,
Where cunning eyes should never trace
The slow course of its under-race.

THE NASTURTIUM FLOWER.

I saw, last night, a ruin gray,
　　An isolated tower,
A work of art, from which decay
Had crumbled portions every day,
　　A feature, every hour;

And o'er it grew a summer vine,
　　A purple Morning Glory,
That hung in many a waving line,
And many a clustering tassel fine,
　　From turrets old and hoary;

And underneath the ruined wall,
　　In moody spirit lying,
I saw the white wave rise and fall,
And heard the sea-bird's mystic call,
　　Far on the waters dying.

The wood upon the sombre hill
　　Its leafy bosom hushes,
And nothing wakes the midnight still,
Save here and there a Whip-po-wil
　　From widely scattered bushes.

I know not if my eyelids fell —
    My pulses were not failing;
I saw the ocean's even swell;
At intervals, my ear could tell
    The lone bird's far-off wailing.

And while I lay, with wandering eye
    O'er Heaven's starry arches,
And watched the meteor shooting by,
And saw the Pleiads holding high
    Their ever-burning torches,

A voice came from the ruin old,
    At first, a pleasant murmur;
And then I heard a story told
In accents stronger, and more bold,
    Of Winter and of Summer.

The Vine said to the Tower gray:
    "My leaves about thee flinging,
Thou shalt not feel the burning day,
Thy rocks shall never waste away
    Where my green arms are clinging.

"Uphold me with thy sturdy hand,
    And lift me from the shadow,
And thou shalt feel thy gray brow fanned
With zephyrs, through its leafy band,
    From fragrant field and meadow.

" I 'll gather all the morning dew
 Within my purple flower,
And when the sun comes up anew,
I 'll wash thy granite bosom true
 With all my silvery shower.

" So tenderly I 'll twine around
 Each fragment, trembling over,
That it shall spurn the colder ground,
And feel itself as sweetly bound
 As lady to her lover.

" I 'll make thy portal emerald-green,
 With here and there a blossom,
And thou shalt have some fairy queen
To come into my leaves, and lean
 Her forehead on thy bosom.

" Oh, I will make thy life so sweet,
 In one delightful Summer,
That pulses in thy heart shall beat
And then — I 'll wither at thy feet,
 And die without a murmur."

Then spoke the cold gray stones, and said:
 " Thy life, sweet Vine, is golden ;
The season all its charms has shed
Upon thy fair and fragile head,
 While I am gray and olden.

"I need not tell thee whence I sprung;
 For yonder craggy mountain
Is not more old, nor yet more young,
Although its brows have frowning hung
 Since Adam, o'er the fountain.

"My form is rude, as thine is fair;
 My limbs are cold and cheerless;
I feel the very summer air
Come searching through me, even where
 Thou cling'st in beauty peerless.

"No zephyr comes but takes away
 A portion of my being;
The gathered dew, that starry spray
Which thou upon my breast would'st lay,
 But aids my life in fleeing.

"The sunshine through thy very leaves
 My particles doth sever;
And while thy tender bosom grieves,
One after one an atom leaves,
 And I am dying ever.

"The summer rain that bids thee live,
 And opens out thy blossom,
Can to my life no freshness give,
But takes away the strength I have
 In passage through my bosom.

" Oh, I have seen a form like thine
  Reach up — how very often ! —
And here its gentle tendrils twine
About this frosty head of mine,
  As thou, my cares to soften.

" And I have seen the Autumn too
  The fairest trellis redden ;
And Winter, pour its breathing through
The very cup that caught the dew,
  And all its powers deaden.

" And one by one their lives have fled,
  As thine will soon be flying ;
And at my feet a fragrant bed
Of withered leaves, and tendrils dead,
  In sorrow will be lying.

" I cannot weep, though all I love,
  The freshest and the fairest,
That on my gray rocks live and move,
Must take the garb that Winter wove
  For that which now thou wearest.

" The Winters come, and come and go,
  And I am here repining ;
I feel alike the sun and snow,
The zephyr or the storms that blow,
  Where thy green arms are twining."

The voices hushed, and silence came,
 A spell upon the Heaven ;
And underneath the Pleiad's flame,
The mantled tower stood the same ;
 The ocean swelled as even.

I prithee, lady, read my dream
 To thine interpretation,
And it shall take that brighter gleam
From thy poetic current stream,
 To music's sweet relation.

In blessing me it must have been,
 At that enchanted hour,
That thou, of fay and blossom kin,
Had left a spirit sleeping in
 The bosom of the flower.

And thus to me in vision thrall
 Came glories without number :
I see the white wave rise and fall,
I hear the sea-bird's mystic call
 In echoes from my slumber.

Ah, unto such a soul as mine
 The gentle fairy's doin'
Was but to tell in softer line,
That thou wert yet a tender vine,
 And I a crumbled ruin !

WINTER NIGHT.

WHEN the soul is weary, weary,
Through these winter days so dreary,
   With their wilderness of white,
There's a charm for such an illness
In the shadow and the stillness
   Of the sober, thoughtful night.

When the earth's green shoots are dying,
And the cold snow o'er them flying —
   Flying all the Winter day,
Then the heart will beat in sadness,
While with strange, fantastic gladness
   The white flakes seem to play.

But the purple Night comes, slowly,
As some abbess, grave and holy,
   Up the still aisles of the sky;
And the red stars troop the arches
With their legions, to the marches
   That are only heard on high.

Then the soul, no longer minion,
Beats the trammels from its pinion,
  Bids its sorrow all adieu ;
And the scarcely dying even,
Sees in yonder tranquil Heaven
  Its white wing cleaving through.

THE LIFE-WAY.

THE axe-man of life, at the Master's decree,
Hath come from the clearing and girdled a tree —
An oak that was leaning in sympathy o'er
The ashes of trees that were girdled before ;
And under our feet, as the passage we tread,
The branches are withered, the blossoms are dead.

Before is a forest, behind is a plain
Where verdure may never be trodden again ;
For, on to the shadow and into the shade,
We follow the way that the woodman has made :
Though sturdy the monarchs, and stately and tall,
The axe of the woodman must girdle them all.

The forest is Life, and the trees are the Years,
The leaves under-foot are the symbols of tears,
And shadows are with us wherever we go,
And spirits are weary and eyelids a-flow ;
For TIME is the woodman, and over his track
The feet of humanity never go back.

*　　*　　*　　*　　*　　*　　-

There are those in the world, who, living too fast,
Have never an eye for the lesson-full past,
But in reaching beyond and peering away,
They trample the bloom that environs to-day,
And suffer with hope, and out of their sorrow
They rush to the ultimate pang of to-morrow.

The pleasures we seek and the jewels we find
Are never before, but are ever behind ;
And carelessly, heedlessly still do we pass
The treasure-full things that go down in the glass ;
For the greed of a greater thing urgeth us on
'Til gem after gem in the life-sand is gone.

Our moments are gold, and the shores of the Past
From whence we have come on the journey too fast,
Are sparkled with riches we never may reach,
That lay in our way as we loitered the beach —
When Hope went ahead with its promises sweet,
We trampled Reality under our feet.

IDEAL PRESENCE.

As bees go over
The seas of clover,
So do my heart-wings go to my lover;
And over the grades
Of murmurous blades,
And over the shimmer and over the shades,
And airy and light
As a fairy's flight,
I follow the arc of the inner sight.

Where a commerce moves
In its iron grooves,
May tarry the clay of the heart that loves;
But over the aisles
Of the iron miles
Must hasten the eye to the eye that smiles;
To the jewel set
In a minaret
The track of its gleam is the truest yet.

THE EASTERN STAR.

I.

In Mason's Hall, with earnest eyes,
  Upon the Chart before me,
I viewed the symboled mysteries
That Masons keep and Masons prize;
I see the arm my brothers wield,
Uplifted with its burnished shield,
  Let fall its shadow o'er me.

II.

My sisters true — in years agone —
  Beyond the waste of water
I see them stand and beck me on:
Sweet RUTH, the gleaner at the dawn;
ELECTA, dear, and MARTHA wait;
Queen ESTHER, in her robes of State;
  And JEPHTHA'S peerless DAUGHTER!

28

III.

JUDGES, xi : 35.

" My father's vow, so fervent made,
   I would not have it broken!
And though my pallid neck be laid
All bare beneath the colder blade,
I 'll give him still a steadfast eye
   And joy, in hearing as I die,
    ' Alas ! my daughter ! ' spoken.
In Heaven's sight my faith I plight,
   And I will break it never :
I 'll trust in *this*, and *this*, and *this*,
   Forever and forever ! "

IV.

RUTH ii : 5.

" The Master in the harvest days
   Shall find me gleaning early ;
The sun shall gild me with his rays
As I go down the reaper ways,
And tho' He ask, ' Whose damsel 's this ? '
I know His great heart cannot miss
   These little hands of barley.
In Heaven's sight my faith I plight,
   And I will break it never :
I 'll trust in *this*, and *this*, and *this*,
   Forever and forever ! "

c*

V.

ESTHER, v : 3.

"I fearless go before the crown
　To move the thorns that fester ;
And though the king himself may frown,
And long to cut God's people down,
I still have faith in such a day
That he will smile and freely say,
　'What wilt thou, proud Queen Esther?'
In Heaven's sight my faith I plight,
　And I will break it never:
I 'll trust in *this*, and *this*, and *this*,
　Forever and forever ! "

VI.

JOHN, xi : 26.

"My faith in Christ no earthly hand
　Can ever move or sever :
Go, take His tidings thro' the land
With cymbals loud and trumpets grand ! ·
For He shall say, 'Believest this?'
And dead shall rise His feet to kiss
　Forever and forever !　　　　·
In Heaven's sight my faith I plight,
　And I will break it never:
I 'll trust in *this*, and *this*, and *this*,
　Forever and forever ! "

VII.

2D EPIS. JOHN, ii : 5.

"Tho' rack and torture come to me —
    To husband, children, mother —
Thro' Jesus' blood I yet shall see
Some glimpses of eternity ;
And far beyond the cross — the grave —
There 's still a hand to bless and save
    For *loving one another.*
In Heaven's sight my faith I plight,
    And I will break it never.:
I 'll trust in *this,* and *this,* and *this,*
    Forever and forever ! "

VIII.

" In virtue's paths my way shall be,
    Where flowers bloom the rarest ;
And all I know, and all I see,
Shall mark a sister's truth in me.
By yon bright star that shines above,
My path I 'll keep, and try to prove,
    Among ten thousand fairest.
In Heaven's sight my faith I plight,
    And I will break it never :   .
I 'll hope in *these,* and *these,* and *these,*
    Forever and forever ! "

LOOKING backward for the glory
   Of a gilded summer dawn,
Down a weary waste of whiteness —
   Down a dreary winter lawn ;
Looking backward for the freshness
   Of a green and sapful June,
Through the sombre brown and crimson
   Of an autumn afternoon ;
Looking backward, down the shadow
   Of an iron-beaten way,
Whence the armored Time came, silent,
   On this animate to-day.
O, it startles human reason,
   O, it withers human pride —
Looking backward, ever backward,
   For the living things that died ;
And the soul that seems immortal
   In the never-breaking gloom,
Hath a presence at the portal
   Of the palace of the tomb.

DEAD FLOWERS.

" Because I wore them for an hour,
    Forever fresh to thee."

THE Rose-bud on thy bosom died —
    O, death, divinely sweet —
Whilst here a poet-heart hath sighed,
To bear to thee its passion tide,
    And perish at thy feet.

The Fuchsia withered on thy brow,
    Amidst thy shining hair ;
Whilst here a soul to earth would bow,
And break its latest altar-vow
    For but one moment there.

O, brow of pearl ! O, breast of snow !
    O, lips of love divine !
The bud hath caught their crimson glow,
And borne thy pulse's tidal flow
    In purple life to mine.

A PIPE AFTER TEA.

BRING me a coal for my old clay pipe —
  A coal that is glowing and red,
    And draw up my chair
    To the fireside there,
  And hasten the children to bed:
We have finished our task and finished our tea,
  And the evening prayer is said.

Now place at the hearth a faggot or two,
  And carry the kettle away;
    I'm thinking, my wife,
    Of the pleasure in life
  We have known this many a day;
For our hearts are warm and our spirits young,
  Though our heads be turning gray.

Ah, now you look, with your knitting, there,
  So cheerful and pleasant, my dear,
    That I feel, full well,
    My old heart swell
  As it did in its bridal gear,
And I know it throbs as faithful still
  In the Autumn-time that's here.

Come back with me to the early day,
 The Spring of our tender love,
  When a fair young bride,
  At the altar-side,
 Looked up to the Heaven above,
And GOD was nigh, and His Summer wind
 Sang joyous in the grove.

Our fathers were there, our mothers too —
 We cherish the blessings they gave ;
  And tears must fall
  To know they 're all
 In the cold and silent grave,
  Where the slow years pass
  In the dropping glass,
 And willows o'er them wave.

But all of us die, and day by day
 We pillow each other to sleep,
  And the tears may rise
  To our saddened eyes
 From the heart in its sorrow deep ;
But GOD hath an eye to the sparrow's fall,
 And the humblest soul will keep.

For two score years we have kept our faith,
 And true to our earliest tryst,
  We have found the goal
  Of a quiet soul,

That many a heart hath missed,
And many a spirit hath wandered away
To the tones we would not list.

Ah, wife, I feel my old blood course
And tingle away in my veins,
When I think how true
Both I and you,
Together, have guided the reins,
With nothing on earth to mar our love,
And fret and bother our brains.

And here we sit, on this Winter night,
A cozy and happy old pair,
And loving as true
As we used to do
When I was young and you were fair,
And the silver thread from the loom of years
Came not in your raven hair.

I shake the coal from my old clay pipe,
For now it is blackened and dead,
And the faggot gone,
And the fire wan,
And the lamp-wick nearly fled,
And the clock, with a nervous stroke, says TEN!
And it's time to go to bed!

UNDER THE PINES.

Night, with her clustering, coronal stars,
Over a world full of passions and wars
    Her quieting wing has spread ;
There 's silence out in these mystical hills —
There 's silence over the voiceful rills,
And Earth, to all of its sorrowful thrills
    In the fever of day, is dead.

O, beautiful Night! sweet season of dreams !
Rich in thy glory and soft in thy gleams,
    How rapidly fleeting thou art!
Throw over my spirit thy mantle of gold,
Let slumber and visions my bosom enfold,
Till all of thine eloquent moments are told
    In the silvery sands of my heart.

Out in the meadow are those who have died,
The stream running still from the wound open wide —
    Oh, I sickened all day at the sight !
Alas! for the heart of its idol denied !
Alas! for the vow of the groom to the bride !
He only may come to her tremulous side
    In the beautiful visions of Night !

D

SHE.

O, COLD are the flakes
That fall in the lakes,
And bitter the winds that be ;
And icy and chill
The minarets still
That stand in the Polar Sea;

But colder than all
Of the flakes that fall,
And the bitterest winds that be —
Than the *Mer de glace*
In the Northern Pass —
Than the Pole itself — is she.

In the amber light
Of the sky, one night,
I tore my bosom apart,
And under a moon
Of the fervid June
Was "offered" to her my heart;

For I tore it out
Of its red redoubt,

And laid it over the pyre,
   Where the torrid heat
   Of its fever-beat
Went, soul to soul, with the fire.

   But never a stone
   To the chisel known
So little of pulse betrayed,
   And the passion lines
   Of her outer signs
Meant — never a word they said.

   O, the glacier stoop .
   Of her shoulders' droop
May show in the night like gold,
   And the lunar fleck
   On her marble neck
A tinge of the blood may hold;

   But never a drop
   Of the venous cup
Can ever the lancet shed :
   The fever has flown —
   The woman is stone,
And the sylph-like thing is dead.

   What the boddice robes
   For her mammal globes
Is only an icy lie ;

Though the lace may rest
On her milk-white breast,
A babe at the place would die!

For colder than all
Of the flakes that fall,
And the bitterest winds that be —
Than the *Mer de glace*
In the Northern Pass —
Than the Pole itself — is she!

HER whiter hand lay lost in mine,
　　The while she turned away
To where the evening's flush of wine
　　Went up the face of day —
"When all these Autumn leaves are shed,
　　And I beyond the sea,
You 'll not forget, O Love," I said,
　　"The faith you 've plighted me?"

Her brown eyes, going outward far,
　　Were silent in reply;
It seemed she thought some early star
　　Would break the shadowed sky;
"When seeds of Spring are harvest grain,
　　And leaves in purple be,
You 'll not forget," I said again,
　　"The faith you 've plighted me?"

And shadows thickened where we stood,
　　And night came on apace;

I saw a tear — the heart's true blood —
   Stand silent on her face
" By these two hands at parting met,
   By sacred tears I see,
I know, dear Love, you 'll not forget
   The faith you 've plighted me."

Then came her full-heart from her eyes,
   Turned, liquidly, to mine —
" Did Eve forget her Paradise
   Beneath another vine ?
No, no," she said, " the waves may fling
   Their whiteness on the sea,
Nor time, nor tide, nor death shall bring
   Forgetfulness to me ! "

  *   *   *   *   *   *

I went where science, learning, art,
   Heaped memorable piles ;
I felt the great world's pulsing heart
   Throb in the Flower Isles ;
I saw the countless soulful eyes
   That sparkle in their dance,
Beneath the rich Italian skies,
   The fruity hills of France ;

The Scottish truth — the Irish grace —
   The German's frugal care —

In every shape the human face,
  And beauty everywhere;
And Summer and the Autumn came,
  And leaves were in their fall —
I held her image here the same,
  An idol over all.

*   *   *   *   *   *

You mark the pale, proud woman there.
  Beneath the astral shine:
Despite such blossoms in her hair
  Her'heart should pulse to mine:
I brought the sunset back to-night
  From far beyond the sea;
I dared not think she held so light
  The faith she plighted me!

I clutched the goblet as a vise,
  And pledged her thus in wine;
May Eve forget her Paradise
  Beneath another vine !
And then I said, the waves may fling
  Their whiteness on the sea,
Nor time, nor tide, nor death shall bring
  Forgetfulness to me !

O, friend ! I trust no siren tongue,
  No human voice or tears;

In all the world I dwelt among,
  No eye had truth like hers.
I pass no more the blighted spot,
  No more the shadows see,
Since she who loved so soon forgot
  The faith she plighted me!

CHARITY.

How many proud people who gather to-day
In chambers of pleasure, at feasts of display,
Who quicken their lips in immaculate wine,
With its typical foam and its sparkle divine,
Have a pang at the heart, or a tear at the eye,
For the woman in rags who is shivering by?

How many to-day in this legion of souls
Who are tracing the pictures that glow in the coals,
Who see in the future their temples arise
As the wonderful homes unto worshipful eyes,
Have pulses awake for the shadowy poor,
Who, white as the marble, enphantom the door?

How many, O GOD! in Thy mercy and grace,
Who are made in Thy form and are stamped with
    Thy face,

Who move on Thy footstool, and graciously live
With light for Thy worship, with power to give,
Have oil for the wounds of the man by the way,
Or bread to be cast on the waters to-day?

O, people whose chambers of crimson and gold
Are astir with the lambs of your own little fold,
Whose feet in their frolic just dimple the bed
Of the burying velvet the little ones tread,
Be still for a season, just hearken the moans
Of the poor little feet that are bare on the stones!

O, people who banquet, and revel, and laugh
In the blood of the grape and the fat of the calf;
When dwelling in plenty and swelling in pride
Your children are petted, and pampered, and plied,
Throw open your casements, and look at the brood
Just over the way, who are crying for food!

O, people in coaches, with liveried things
That wait in the glitter of tinsel and rings,
That come at your becking and go at your will —
All creatures of Mammon—God's images still!—
Sink back in your cushions and hide you in shame
From the piteous eyes of the paupered and lame!

O, mistress of fashion! O, master of gold!
Far hidden in furs from the sting of the cold —
As your spirits go out and your ecstasy swells

At the sight of the snow and the sound of the bells,
Do you mind that the widow is wanting a cloak —
That her chimney is bleak in a city of smoke?

Come out of your casings, O, armor-clad souls,
That live in the tinkle of ewers and bowls;
Come out from the sight of your carpeted feet
With pity for those that are bare in the street:
Come, open your coffers, in mercy, to-day,
For the little ones crying just over the way!

Step out of your coaches and cutters, O, fools
That sneer at the wretches that dwell in the pools;
Step out, and for once in the bountiful year
Have eyes that can see and have ears that can
    hear;
Step out from your cushions of revel and shame —
Go comfort the widow, go pity the lame!

O, there's nothing at all in this region below
So hollow and dead as their tinsel and show;
When people who shimmer in glory and gold
Are blind to the beings that dwell in the cold;
When lights from their windows, that dazzle the
    poor,
See most of true virtue outside of the door!

O, blessings for people, who, feasting to-day,
Have thought of the little ones over the way;

Whose spirits, grown large at the board and the
        hearth,
Cry welcome, to all the distressed of the earth!
O, blessings for people, who, hearing their moans,
Have lifted the bare-footed out of the stones!

SEVENTY.

THE sad Sixty-nine in the midnight has gone,
And Seventy comes in his chariot on ;
With light in his eye and a flush in his face,
He enters the course and is in for the race.
A fever of being, a fullness of joy
Is throbbing the pulse of the animate boy.
'Tis a glorious hope that his spirit reveals
In the crack of his whip and the rush of his wheels.

*   *   *   *   *   *

But life is a mockery — common decay
Is big in the womb of the promising day ;
For death hath a touch at the heart of the corn
Ere light on the silk of its tassel is born ;
And never a flower abandons the dust
But foldeth a germ of the cankering rust ;
And even the beautiful, bountiful year
That cometh to-day in its infancy here,
Is typed in the life of ephemeral bloom,
For he driveth his chariot on to the tomb.

E

In the glow of a purple October —
   The nut-dropping time of the year —
When leaves have a rustle of splendor,
   And branches in silver appear,
As cometh the sun to the Sabbath,
   Up out of the Orient hills,
A sense of an Infinite Being
   The whole of humanity fills.

Man sees in the passage of seasons,
   The regular transit of days,
How great is Thy goodness, Jehovah!
   How wondrous, O GOD, are Thy ways!
The steeple-bells over the churches
   That dot, in their whiteness, the land,
Elate. at the glad Sabbath morning,
   Ring out in a symphony grand;
And homes that are sprinkled with children
   A story of happiness tells,

When faces grow bright at the music
   That flows from the Sabbath School bells.

Now out of the lane and the by-way,
   And out of the alley and street,
With. murmurous mingle of voices
   And musical patter of feet,
The children of *all* of the people —
   The humble in state and the high,
The rich in their Astrachan wrappings,
   The poor in their woolen — go by.

And in. at the arch of the chapel,
   Along in the sanctified aisles,
They gather like earliest blossoms
   That Spring in her beauty beguiles ;
And there, at the foot of the altar —
   A ground that is *even* at last —
The hearts of the children are measured
   By Heaven's true standard of caste.

The bells of the Sabbath are ringing
   Alike for the rich and the poor,
And open the mine of the Bible
   To all who are seeking its store :
No prince at the zenith of power,
   With nations on suppliant knees,
Hath gems in his coronal decking
   That sparkle in fervor like these.

Come hither, O children, and gather
  The jewels GOD scatters to-day ;
Here 's Honor, and Virtue, and Mercy,
  The riches that never decay ;
Here 's knowledge that 's free to the orphan,
  The child of the widow may learn —
The prince and the pauper together
  May in at the vestibule turn.

Come, children, glad-eyed and white-hearted,
  And join in an anthem of praise ;
Thank GOD for the voice in the steeple
  That heralds His holiest days ;
Thank GOD for the boon of the Bible,
  The blessed Redeemer of men,
The glorious plan of salvation.
  Revealed in the beautiful Ten.

Away with sectarian uses,
  The narrow confinements of creed ;
The little one's heart is a garden
  Where Jesus should scatter the seed.
Teach GOD as a merciful Father,
  The source and the fountain of love ;
Not feared for His might, and the power
  He wields in the kingdom above,
But honored and glorified ever
  For Charity, Mercy, and Love,
The jewels to seek in the Bible
  And wear to the kingdom above.

These grey-bearded men of the city,
　Worn out in the service of trade,
Their foot-way, borne down from the sunlight,
　Is bent to the valley of shade ;
And stories of struggle and sorrow
　The lines in their faces can tell,
Since light-hearted children together
　They answered the Sabbath School bell.

And often and often at midnight
　Their memory goes to the past,
To wander again in the flowers
　That GOD in their passage had cast ;
And up from the glory of childhood,
　In mystical melody swells
A sound that endureth forever —
　The song of the Sabbath Day bells.

TYPE AND TIME.

THAT stern old man, the Harvester.
  Who garners in the years,
Whose passage up the fields of space
  A path of death appears ;
Whose way is in the early grain
  Ere yet its golden hue,
. And bended head, and parting husk,
  Invite the sickle through ;

That cold old man, whose arteries,
  At Mercy's plaint, congeal
And harden, that they may but show
  The blood's organic steel —
He feels no pity, knows no shame,
  Nor spares nor passes o'er
An atom in the widening plain
  That, trackless, lies before.

He turns not back, but onward still,
  With steady, tireless sweep,

His burnished scythe goes through the realm
　　Forevermore to reap ;
No Ruth of Moab in his wake
　　With tender hands may glean,
Nor stem nor stalk shall stand for her
　　Where iron Time has been.

But stolid eye and tuneless ear
　　Shall quicken at a sound
That floats above the reaper sphere,
　　And spurns the harvest-ground ;
For Time shall note, beyond the dust
　　Of men and nations wrecked,
The stately tread of Genius,
　　And the march of Intellect.

Whoso hath marked the lives of men,
　　Their better words and deeds,
May point some flower blossoming
　　Above the trammel weeds ;
Some growth hath struggled out the arms
　　That undertwine the way,
And lifts its scented splendor
　　In the ardent upper day.

Though blight and blast may fell the stalk
　　In seasons urging by,
The essence of the flower still
　　Is floating on the sky ;

And free, beyond the reach of death,
  Upon the arch sublime,
The souls of men of Intellect
  And Genius conquer Time.

Go back along the shadow-days,
  And down their cycles run,
And mark the lights from human lives
  Since human lives begun :
Though countless legions in the throng
  Were stars that early set,   ·
The grand old planets of the past
  Are at the zenith yet.

From out the darkness of an age
  That gave their genius birth,
They rose above the atmosphere
  And battled down the earth ;
And in the space, from every clime,
  And every class, are some
Who prove how under-gravity
  Is grandly overcome.

So let us live, and act, and be,
  That after-time may tell
We were not in the reaper-way,
  Nor by the sickle fell ;
But upward, over all that die,
  By force of human will,

We cut a passage to the sky
    And hold the æther still.

*   *   *   *   *   *

On those who gather here to-day,
    Some lights, that ever show,
Have come to shed their glory-ray
    From out the long-ago :
The first old masters of an Art,
    Ere Genius yet was ripe,
Who threw the cruder stylus down
    To greet the coming Type ;

Who from the cells of hooded monks, ..
    And sacrist scribes, and clerks,
Were free to bear the outer world
    The magic of their works ;
Who tore the vail of mystery
    From small Khorassans then
That swayed the world with vellum scraps
    Of wisdom from the pen.

The German Koster, first of all,
    Whose carven letters came
And gave the acts of noble men
    To glory and to fame ;
Whose spirit, from the narrow groove
    That circumscribed his kind,
Was bold to break the barrier
    And poach the fields of mind.

The common chain that ignorance
  And superstition bound,
His light ambition scorned to wear
  Upon the trodden ground ;
And men were taught forevermore
  That better path to climb,
When KOSTER sent the Bible up
  The avenues of Time.

Though long ago his parchment sheets,
  And vellum scrolls, and leaves
Were gathered by the Harvester
  And lie among the sheaves,
We lift the science of his thought
  From out the rubbish lost,
With honor to old GUTTENBERG
  And gratitude to FAUST.

Where'er the cunning Type is known —
  Where'er the magic page
Is stamped with living characters
  That photograph the age,
The massive forms of GUTTENBERG,
  Of FAUST, and SCHŒFFER too,
Shall stalk the aisles of learning
  And the paths of genius through.

These are the planet-stars that shine
  For those who follow still

The science-way that leaves the vale
  And takes the stubborn hill ;
These are the patron-saints — the gods
  Of energy and worth,
That point us from Apprenticeship
  To Mastery on earth.

And down the sparkled arch that bends
  Above these darker years,
We hail the risen splendor
  Of our later pioneers ;
The noble FRANKLIN of our own,
  Whose hand of usefulness
Was first to clutch the thunderbolt
  And draw the lever-press.

The simple beauty of his life —
  The smooth and even pace
With which he took the upper way
  And won the honor race,
Have left, through reaching history
  And ever-ringing fame,
The civil world electrified
  And nervous with his name.

We hold the greatness of his brain,
  His openness and truth,
The highest model for our men,
  The noblest for our youth ;

The brawn-armed daily laborer —
  The ermined of the State
May find, in FRANKLIN's excellence,
  A life to emulate.

And after him, above the verge,
  Our firmament can show
The advent of another star —
  The scintillating HOE !
The hot sheets from his cylinders
  O'er all the land are spread,
.To tell the world how Intellect
  And Genius are not dead.

White-winged and free, across the sea
  His seeds of labor fly,
And men must know, where'er they go,
  How Genius cannot die ;
For all the soil of fertile brains
  With labor-seeds are rife —
They germinate in fields of fame,
  And in the sands of life.

As long as Christian temples bear
  Their turrets to the sun —
As long as in our cycle-lives
  The sands of Fame shall run,
So long shall human hearts be glad,
  And human voices bless

The master-hands that wrought the Type
And reared the magic Press.

*   *   *   *   *   *

For us, who stand as Signal-men,
  Along the army track,
And onward wave the messages,
  From flags that lessen back,
How meet it is that arm, and eye,
  Should steady be, and true,
To guard the honor of the post,
  And speed the signal through.

We hold the symbol of a cause,
  A power in our hands,
To point the army-march, and shape
  The destiny of lands ;
To good, or ill, we guide the world,
  By virtue of our trust —
For good, we lift the signal high —
  For ill, it trails the dust.

When, here and there, a veteran
  And leader in the corps,
Is signalled from the angel flags
  That flit the silent shore,
He musters out of human strife,
  And treads the courts of fate —
Our HARNEY's through the vestibule,
  Our PRENTICE at the gate.

F

God keep us in the goodly track,
   That leaves the ill behind !
God turn us to the flower-way
   Of love for humankind !
God give us grace to wield the PEN,
   And so direct the PRESS,
That we may point our fellow-men,
   To ever-blessedness !

And TIME may keep his steady sweep
   Throughout the fields of earth,
And in the maze of autumn days
   May fell the latest birth ;
But human souls have higher goals,
   Where reapers never dare,
And men shall rise beyond the skies,
   To shine forever there.

SWEETHEART.

Sweetheart—I call you sweetheart still
  As in your window's laced recess,
When both our eyes were wont to fill,
  One year ago, with tenderness.
I call you sweetheart by the law
  Which gives me higher right to feel,
Though I be here in Malaga,
  And you in far Mobile.

I mind me when, along the bay
  The moon-beams slanted all the night;
When on my breast your dark locks lay,
  And in my hand, your hand so white;
This scene the summer night-time saw,
  And my soul took its warm anneal
And bore it here to Malaga
  From beautiful Mobile.

The still and white magnolia grove
  Brought winged odors to your cheek,

Where my lips seared the burning love
    They could not frame the words to speak;
Sweetheart, you were not ice to thaw;
    Your breast was neither stone nor steel;
I count to-night, at Malaga,
    Its throbbings at Mobile.

What matter if you bid me now
    To go my way for others' sake?
Was not my love-seal on your brow
    For death, and not for days to break?
Sweetheart, our trothing holds no flaw;
    There was no crime and no conceal,
I clasp you here in Malaga,
    As erst in sweet Mobile.

I see the bay-road, white with shells,
    I hear the beach make low refrain,
The stars lie flecked like asphodels
    Upon the green, wide water-plain—
These silent things as magnets draw,
    They bear me hence, with rushing keel
A thousand miles from Malaga,
    To matchless, fair Mobile.

Sweetheart, there is no sea so wide,
    No time in life, nor tide to flow,
Can rob my breast of that one bride
    It held so close a year ago.

I see again the bay we saw ;
　I hear again your sigh's reveal,
I keep the faith at Malaga
　I plighted at Mobile.

.

.

I saw a star fall from its home
In Heaven's blue and boundless dome,
    To gleam no more ;
I saw a wave with snowy crest
Thrown from the Ocean's stormy breast,
    Upon the shore.

I saw a rose of perfect bloom
Bend, fading to its wintry tomb
    In silent grief;
I saw a living oak, but now,
Touched by the storm, with shattered bough
    And withered leaf.

The star had shone tnro' countless years,
And shed its rays like virgin tears,
    So pure and bright,
That earth scarce knew the holy thrall,
And only sighed to see it fall
    And fade in night.

The wave h_id wandered to and fro,
With Ocean's ebb and Ocean's flow,
    From pole to pole,
Till here upon the nameless strand
It sank beneath the thirsty sand,
    Its final goal!

The rose sprang from a fallen seed,
And smiled above the graceless weed,
    To greet the sun;
But 'neath the Winter's chilling breath,
The lovely flow'rets' race to death
    Was quickly run.

The living oak, with noble shade,
Had stood the monarch of the glade,
    Thro' ages long;
But rifted by the lightning's glare,
His sturdy arms grew brown and bare,
    And were not strong.

And these are types of human lives;
Man lives a little while and thrives,
    But withers fast.
He sees a thousand lovely gleams,
But wastes his life away in dreams,
    And falls at last.

THE PATH.

Just by the road we are journeying fast,
    Down to the Lake of Tears,
A blind old man has tottered at last,
Out of the Present into the Past,
    Over the brink of years.

What were his virtues, what were his crimes,
    Nobody cares to-day;
Once he was ours — now he is Time's —
For lives are but as murmuring chimes,
    Coming and going away.

Up on the hill there 's a patter of feet —
    A voice in the flowers wild;
Carelessly down to the busy street,
Many to pass, and many to meet,
    Rambles a little child.

68

This is "the dead man's son and heir"
    Coming along the road ;
He gathers the lightest treasures there,
The violet bloom and crocus fair,
    Bearing a childish load.

Soon he will be in the hurrying crowd,
    Pushing his way ahead —
Some of them broken — some of them bowed,
Some for the altar and some for the shroud,
    Some who are leading and led.

Soon in the way to the Lake of Tears,
    The little one's feet must go ;
For thorns are thick in the path of years,
And the way to death is a way of fears,
    All down to the silent flow.

THE BIVOUAC.

A SOLDIER lay on the frozen ground,
With only a blanket tightened around
    His weary and wasted frame;
Down at his feet, the fitful light
Of fading coals in the freezing night
Fell as a mockery on the sight,
    A heatless, purple flame.

All day long, with his heavy load,
Weary and sore, in the mountain road,
    And over the desolate plain;
All day long, through the crusted mud,
Over the snow, and through the flood,
Marking his way with a track of blood
    He followed the winding train.

Nothing to eat at the bivouac
But a frozen crust in his haversack —

The half of a comrade's store —
A crust, that, after a longer fast,
Some pampered spaniel might have passed,
Knowing that morsel to be the last
 That lay at his master's door.

No other sound on his slumber fell
Than the lonesome tread of the sentinel —
 That equal, measured pace —
And the wind that came from the cracking pine,
And the dying oak, and the swinging vine,
In many a weary, weary line,
 To his pale and hollow face.

But the soldier slept, and his dreams were bright
As the rosy glow of his bridal-night,
 With the angel on his breast;
For he passed away from the wintry gloom
To the softened light of a distant room,
Where a cat sat purring upon the loom,
 And his weary heart was blest.

His children came, two blue-eyed girls,
With laughing lips and sunny curls,
 And cheeks of ruddy glow;
And the mother pale, but lovely now,
As when, upon her virgin brow
He proudly scaled his early vow,
 In summer, long ago.

But the *reveillé* wild, in the morning gray,
Startled the beautiful vision away,
    As a frightened bird in the night;
And it seemed to the soldier's misty brain
But the shrill *tattoo* that sounded again,
And he turned with a dull, uneasy pain,
    To the camp-fires' dying light.

HEART LESSONS.

I HAD no design in passing —
  I was walking rather late —
I did not dream that ROSA GRAY
  Was standing at the gate ;

And when the cloud passed over,
  And the moon revealed her there,
With its ripple on her bosom
  And its shimmer in her hair,

I was startled at the glory
  And the suddenness of light,
That had silvered up the arches
  Over all the aisles of night.

I had kept my passion hidden ;
  I had held it deathly still
Through the vigor of my manhood,
  Through the power of my will.

G

Oh, the pride in being master!
  Oh, the dread of being slave!
Better wear the crimson fever
  In a by-way to the grave.

Better hold it — hide it downward,
  Though the fibrous, vital man
From the inner heat's expansion
  Into baser metal ran.

Better feel the slowest fusion
  Of the being's finer parts,
Than to show the garish colors
  And the flame of common hearts.

But this sudden, white appearance
  At the gate of ROSA GRAY,
Drove my real nature backward —
  Drove my stronger self away.

Standing, queenly, where the moon-glow
  Brought its finish to her cheek,
Where the star-eyes saw her breast-swells
  At the boddice-margin break,

Some entire unknown sensation,
  From the heart's entangled wild,
Broke amain upon my life-strings,
  And o'erswept me as a child.

. She was looking far to seaward,
  And her outline shone so clear
That she seemed a chiseled SILENCE,
  Cut from silver, leaning there.

And the near Egyptian Lily,
  Bending from its marble vase,
Might be fairer for her whiteness,
  Might be rarer for her grace.

She was looking far to seaward,
  And the moon-path, silver laid,
For the passage of her vision
  To the outer world, was made.

She was lost in dreamy poems
  To the ever verseful sea,
And the dimmest stars were nearer
  Than her soul was unto me.

I approached her like a coward;
  For the under-lying dew
Scarcely sparkled at my foot-fall
  In its noiseless passage through.

" Rosa Gray," I said, and touched her
  From her meditative sleep —
" What of all this coral labor :
  Will it overcome the deep ?

" Mark you yonder reef, unbroken
   Through the foam-line of its length :
Has this boundless spread of water,
   Or the insect, greater strength ?

" Mark you how the brine beats ever
   Up the still and steadfast wall :
Do the spray-drops gather marble,
   That they whiten as they fall?

" There are grottos, arches, towers,
   Cities, islands building on :
Will not Time proclaim a triumph
   When the Ocean shall be gone?

" Come, now, ROSA GRAY, and listen :
   Once my heart was all a sea,
And the thought-ships furrowed o'er it,
   Bringing treasures unto me ;

" Fair white sails from isles of learning,
   Bringing knowledge unto me ;
I was master of its commerce,
   I was monarch of the sea.

" I could feel the waves go outward,
   And the wind-share cutting free
Through the white-enameled furrows
   Of my great, expanding sea.

"You began your labor early
    In my heart-deeps, Rosa Gray,
And my ships, and waves, and ocean,
    Long ago have passed away.

"So you fill me now, and sway me,
    With the cunning of your skill;
I have neither force nor reason,
    I have neither way nor will.

"Speak me truthful words, O mistress ɪ
    In this fever of my mood;
Let my heart-valves force the chalice,
    Be it poison, down my blood!"

You have seen a twig inclining,
    Where, the liquid crystal found,
Kept the murmur of its music
    In the alleys underground;

So I thought to find her spirit,
    So I sought to catch her tone,
Where the magic of my circle
    Was the compass of her zone.

And Rosa Gray looked outward
    Once again toward the waves,
And her eyes came o'er with pity
    As the dews come over leaves;

G *

And my own eyes burning in them,
  Burning through the glassy flow,
Saw her real being shrinking
  In the darkness far below.

Little need for her to utter,
  Little need for her to move —
Friend, I came not in the margin
  Of the shadow of her love.

Mark you, now, I 'm looking backward,
  Somewhat further than it seems,
Where the real things that met us
  Take the portraiture of dreams.

There was no design in passing —
  I repeat here what I said —
I but followed where the genius
  Of my meditation led.

It was well I came upon her
  In that mystic, latter noon,
When my heart gave off its burthen
  As the cloud went off the moon.

It was well to yield my purpose
  To the sway of impulse then ;
It was well to bring my greatness
  To the plane of common men.

It was meet that I, a beggar,
  Trailing ermine as a king,
In her real, regal presence
  Should appear the lower thing.

What is human pride and purpose
  But a passion at the most?
Men are haunted through ambition,
  And their vanity 's the ghost.

For the lessons and the knowledge
  That she gave me, ROSA GRAY,
I would cast the garnered learning
  Of a former life away.

And I mind me often, often,
  In my wanderings of late,
Of the figure standing silent
  In the halo at the gate.

And I tread the pathway backward,
  To that mystic, latter noon,
When my heart gave off its burthen
  As the cloud went off the moon.

TIME AT THE SOUTH.

In the shade of the pool, where the queen-lily dips,
With the dew of the night on her beautiful lips;

Where blossoms the orange, where bloometh the rose,
And the bright oleander and jessamine blows;

Tread lightly, tread softly, O merciful Time,
O'er the land of the sun, and the lemon, and lime;

For leaves of the flowers so faded and strewn
Were fair in the morning and fallen at noon.

Go back to the plane of your ice-hidden lakes —
Go back with your breath of the frost and the flakes;

Go Northward, O season of Winter and gloom,
From the emerald South and its odorous bloom.

O, the purple dead leaves that environ the ways
Of the genius of Time in its passage of days;

O, the late-fallen leaves and the withering grass —
How they rustle, and gather, and people the pass!

O, better to die and be hidden away,
Than to live in the circle and sight of decay.

Our metals of life in their crucibles run
When the pulses are red in the glow of the sun.

But come to the South with the ice of your heel,
And the channels are still and the currents congeal.

Go backward, O Winter, go back to the lakes,
With your withering frost and your wandering flakes.

  * * * * * *

The bush is borne down and the blossom is shed,
And we gather to-day at the grave of the dead.

The corse that is stark, and the body that's cold,
Is a link of the past to be lost in the mold;

And armies may file to the sepulchre plain
To laurel the bier of the body that's slain;

But never again, at the death of the years,
Will the heart of the Southron be lavish of tears.

Go seek in the far-reaching fields of his land,
For the shade of his column and capital grand;

Go look for the mosque of his worship and pride;
Go look for his brother — go look for his bride;

Go look for all things he has cherished and loved—
The garden he haunted, the valley he roved —

And the desolate track, and the ravens that fly,
Will tell that the fount of the Southron is dry.

Time was, when a sentinel stood at the gate,
And guarded the annals and altars of state;

When the gleam of his eye and the glare of his blade
Kept the wolf in the covert afar and afraid;

When the good and the pure, and the noble and true,
Were all in the land that the sentinel knew:

Time was when the tyrant would blanch in the sight
Of the column and arch of our temple of right,

When the marbles of state in their purity stood,
That our fathers had builded and hallowed in blood;

But time is long gone with the sands of the glass,
When *honor* was watchword, and *virtue* the pass.

Go banish the dust from your lexicons old,
Ye people that glitter and seek to be gold;

Go back to the schools of your earlier days,
For their lessons of truth, and their patriot lays;

Go study the greatness, that tried in the fires,
Shone bright in the glory that covered your sires;

Go feel in the spell that encircles their graves
That tyrants and cowards are meaner than slaves.

Oh, men of the nation — oh, rulers and kings,
Do ye know that your riches and powers have wings?

Do ye know that the ashes ye scatter and spurn,
Must quicken in time and arise from the urn?

Do ye know that the gates where ye gather your tolls,
Are peopled with things that have pulses and souls?

Do ye dare, from your source in the dust and the clods,
To covet the robes and the thrones of the gods?

Ye may look at the waves that go out on the sea,
And learn from the past what your future will be;

For the ocean is broad, and the wave in its track,
Must follow, and follow, and never come back.

Ye are like to the waves that are gathered and tost,
And driven to sea, to be scattered and lost —

In the morn, ere the scent of the roses is o'er,
Ye may sleep in the cove and the calm of the shore;

Ye may toy in the isles at the mellower noon,
With your feathery spray and its murmurous tune;

But evening must come from the shadow at last,
With a garment of gloom and a gathering blast.

DOUBLE LIFE.

OVER pools of purest water,
  Lying silent, there will come,
Soon, or late, the green enamel
  Of a quickened herbage-scum;
Taking color from the vesture
  That the margin grasses wear,
Till it hides the lambent sparkle
  Of the liquid crystal there.

So the poet-nature shadows
  All its glory with a cloud,
That the soul-light may not dazzle
  In the ordinary crowd;
So they hide their real beings,
  So they live and act a part,
Making nature but an adjunct
  To the perfectness of art.

Oh, I hate this outward seeming,
  This unreal, double-life,

Where the face is full of quiet
  While the heart is full of strife ;
For our latent inner-currents
  Would to other currents run,
Though the waters of the spirit
  May be hidden from the sun.

We may live upon the surface,
  We may wear the mantle green,
And among tho outer beings,
  Be as outer beings seen ;
But the spheres of souls magnetic
  Are beyond the common thrall,
And the true life of the poet
  Pulseth under, after all.

THE LITTLE BOY GUIDING THE PLOW.

When a bugle-note rang in the quivering trees,
  And a drum beat the nation to arms,
Our people came up from the shore of the seas,
  And away from their blue-mountain farms;
All stalwart and strong as the hardy old pines,
  Or the wave-breaking rocks of the shore,
They came in their long gleaming columns and lines,
  Till the bugle-note sounded no more.
There are hearts in the ranks, as light as the foam;
  There are those of a gloomier brow;
And some who have left but a mother at home,
  With her little boy guiding the plow.

There are silver-haired men, the tide in their veins
  Leaping down the red alleys of youth,
All fresh as the water-fall thrown to the plains,
  And as pure as the beautiful truth;
There are sons too, and sires — the old and the
      young —
  In the midnight and morning of life,

Who came from the hills and the valleys among,
　To be first in the glorious strife;
And many, how many beneath the blue dome,
　Are bending in solitude now,
To plead for the weal of a mother at home,
　And her little boy guiding the plow!

Oh, the pang of his heart, and the keenest of all
　That a wandering father may know,
Is the vision of home with its agony-call,
　Its hunger and shivering woe;
And who would not chafe in the sacredest chain
　At a memory bitter as this,
Though he knew in his heart that each moment of
　　pain
　Would but hallow his future to bliss?
And who would not weep in a vision of gloom,
　When the Evil One whispered him how
The toil grew apace to the mother at home,
　And her little boy guiding the plow?

But courage, keep courage, oh, parent away!
　Be noble, and faithful, and brave!
And the midnight shall pass, and the glorious day
　Shall be shed over tyranny's grave!
Though a desolate thing is a fenceless farm,
　And as dreary, a furrowless field,
Still, God in his mercy shall strengthen the arm
　Of the little boy asking a yield;

And the stubbornest clay shall be as the loam,
  When the patriot spirit shall bow,
And ask for a friend to the mother at home,
  And her little boy guiding the plow.

Oh, God will be kind to the needy and poor
  Who shall suffer from tyranny's hand;
His foot-print shall be by the loneliest door,
  And his bounty shall cover the land;
And broken the glebe in the valley and mead,
  Where the poorest and weakest shall be,
And plenty shall spring of the promising seed,
  Till a people shall live to be free;
And never, oh, never shall tyranny come,
  With iron-bound bosom and brow —
May God give him back to the mother at home,
  And her little boy guiding the plow!

THE FLOWER GRAVES.

FROM the fields that underlie us,
   Down the flowered South's incline,
Where the vintage of the battles
   Took a deeper glow than wine;
When the early green of summer,
   Winning out the smitten gaze,
Caught, from war, a sudden crimson,
   As of later autumn days;
Where the tangled, trodden grasses,
   And the fragment blades and shells,
All the story of the struggle,
   More than eloquently tells;

From the salients and the centres,
   And the points of jealous guard,
Where the trees and earth with missiles
   Bearing death were deepest scarred;
Where the tempered blade was needed,
   And the gallant arm to wield,
For the honor and the glory
   And the guidance of the field;

In the surge and edge of carnage,
  In the battle's tidal flow,
At the focus of the conflict,
  At the colors of the foe —
There we sought, and *there* we found them —
  In the clotted field and fen —
Found the relics, and the shadows,
  Of our grand and god-like men.

Meet it is, oh widow — mother ! —
  From this sweet, prolific May,
Thus to bear its living garlands
  Through the winter of your way.

Meet it is, O men and brothers !
  Here amid the fallen great,
These to glorify and honor
  As the noblest of your State.

In the shadow of a column,
  Bearing upward to the day,
Yonder carven marble semblance
  Of the ever-living CLAY,
Well it is that they should slumber,
  Who, beneath his power-tone,
From the cradle-time of being,
  Into patriots had grown ;
Who were early taught his lessons,
  And to noble paths inclined

· By his scorn of crawling spirits,
　And the narrow grooves of mind ;
Who were taught the worth of freedom,
　And the glory of such graves
As should come before the shackles,
　And the curse of being slaves.

Bring your garlands here, O sister,
　For the brother who is free,
Who to brutal pomp and power
　Never bent a servile knee.

For the cause in which he suffered,
　And the hearth and home-lands gone,
Yet his ashes rise in witness
　At the courts of after-dawn —
Let his banner bear the record
　Of an impulse in his blade,
When the red track down an army
　Told the havoc he had made.

Such an even-handed justice
　As the nation's cannot move,
There will be in that tribunal,
　At the golden bar above.

Bring the rose and lily hither,
　And the May-time's early bloom ;
Let us conquer now, with flowers,
　·All the legions of the tomb ;

Let the green and living garlands
  Over all the mounds be shed,
As a token that the heroes
  Underlying, are not dead.

Keep them fresh, O eyes of beauty,
  With the moisture of your tears,
That their souls may haunt the flowers
  Down your summer-way of years.
Keep them fresh with darling kisses;
  Let them feel your bosom-sigh,
And the thousand years of glory
  Shall not see the Southrons die.

FALLEN.

THE iron voice from yonder spire
  Has hush'd its hollow tone,
And midnight finds me lying here,
  In silence and alone.

The still moon through my window
  Sheds its soft light on the floor,
With a melancholy paleness,
  I have never seen before ;

And the summer wind comes to me
  With its sad Æolian lay,
As if burthened with the sorrows
  Of a weary, weary day ;

But the moonlight cannot soothe me
  Of the sickness here within,
And the sad wind takes no portion
  From my bosom's weight of sin.

Yet my heart and all its pses
　　Seem so quietly to rest,
That I scarce can feel ther beating
　　In my arms, or in my b'ast:

These rounded limbs are rting now
　　So still upon the bed,
That one would think, to se me here,
　　That I was lying dead.

What if 'twere so?　Whatf I died
　　As I am lying now,
With something like to vine's calm
　　Upon this pallid brow?

What if I died to-night?　Ah, now
　　This heart begins to bet —
A fallen wretch, like me, ɔ pass
　　From earth, so sadly sɣet!

Yet am I calm! — as calɪ as clouds
　　That slowly float and frm,
To give their burthen-tea in some
　　Unpitying winter storm

As calm as great Sahara
　　E'er the simoom sweeɪ its waste —
As the ocean, e'er the blows
　　All its miles of beachɪave laced.

Still, still, have no tears to shed;
  These eylids have no store —
The founta once within me,
  A fountai is no more.

The moon one looks on me now,
  The pale nd dreamful moon;
She smiles oon my wretchedness,
  Through a the night's sweet noon.

What if I dil to-night — within
  These gildl, wretched walls,
Upon whose rimson tapestry
  No eye of irtue falls.

What would i soulless inmates do
  When they ad found me here,
With cheek to white for passion's smile,
  Too cold fo passion's tear?

Ah! one woul come, and from these arms
  Unclasp the auble bands;
Another, wrenc the jewels from
  My fairer, witer hands.

This splendid rbe, another's form
  Would grace, oh, long before
The tender moc-beam shed again
  Its silver on ie floor.

And when they'd laid me down in earth
  Where pauper graves are made.
Beneath no drooping willow-tree
  In angel-haunted shade,

Who'd come and plant a living vine
  Upon a wretched grave?
Who'd trim the tangled grasses wild
  No summer wind could wave?

Who would raise a stone to mark it
  From ruder graves around,
That the foot-fall of the stranger
  Might be soft upon the ground?

No stone would stand above me there —
  No sadly bending tree,
No hand would plant a myrtle vine
  Above a wretch like me.

What if I died to-night! — and when
  To-morrow's sun had crept
Where late the softer moonlight
  In its virgin beauty slept,

They'd come and find me here — oh, who
  Would weep to see me dead?
Who'd bend the knee of sorrow
  By a pulseless wanton's bed?

There's one would come — *my mother!*
  God bless the angel band
That bore her, ere her daughter fell,
  To yonder quiet land!

Thank God for all the anthem-songs
  That gladdened angels sung,
When my mother went to heaven,
  And I was pure and young!

And there's another too would come —
  A man upon whose brow
My shame hath brought the winter snow
  To rest so heavy now.

Ah! he would come with bitter tears
  All burning down his cheek,—
Had *reason's* kingdom stronger been
  When *virtue* grew so weak!

My sisters and my brothers all,
  Thank God! are far away!
They'll never know how died the one
  That mingled in their play;

They'll never know how wretchedly
  Their darling sister died,
The one who smiled whene'er they smiled,
  Who cried whene'er they cried.

I

For him that sought a spotless hand.
  And lives to know my shame,
In such a place I'd tear the tongue
  That dared to speak his name.

The cold sea-waves run up the sand
  In undulating swells,
And backward to the ocean turn
  When they have kissed the shells;

So, there's a torrent in my breast,
  And I can feel its flow
Rush up in crimson billows
  On a beach as fair as snow;

And backward, backward to my heart,
  The ocean takes its tide,
My cheeks and lips left bloodless all,
  And cold, as if I died!

I'm all alone to-night! How strange
  That I should be alone!
This splendid chamber seems to want
  Some *roué's* passion-tone!

Yon soulless mirror, with its smooth
  And all untarnished face,
Sees not these jewelled arms to-night,
  In their unchaste embrace—

FALLEN.

Oh, I have fled the fever
  Of that heated, crowded hall,
Where I might claim the highest-born
  And noblest of them all;

Where I might smile upon them now
  With easy, wanton grace,
Which subdues the blood of virtue
  That would struggle in my face.

I hate them all — I scorn them,
  As they scorn me in the street;
I could spurn away the pressure
  That my lips too often meet;

I could trample on the lucre
  That their passion never spares:
They robbed me of a heritage
  Of greater price than theirs.

They can never give me back again
  What I have thrown away,
The brightest jewel woman wears
  Throughout her little day!

The brightest, and the only one,
  That from the cluster riven,
Shuts out forever woman's heart
  From all its hopes of Heaven!

What if I died to-night? — and died
  As I am lying here!
There's many a green leaf withered
  Ere autumn comes to sear;

There's many a dew-drop shaken down
  Ere yet the sunshine came,
And many a spark hath died before
  It wakened into flame.

What if I died to-night, and left
  These wretched bonds of clay
To seek beyond this hollow sphere
  A brighter, better day?

What if my soul passed out, and sought
  That haven of the blest
"Where the wicked cease from troubling,
  The weary are at rest"?

Would angels call me from above,
  And beckon me to come
And join them in their holy songs
  In that eternal home?

Would they clasp their hands in gladness
  When they saw my soul set free,
And point—beside my mother's —
  To a place reserved for me?

Would they meet me as a sister,
  As one of precious worth
Who had gained a place in Heaven
  By holiness on earth?

O God! I would not have my soul
  Go out upon the air
With all its weight of wretchedness,
  To wander, where — oh, where?

MIDNIGHT BELLS.

Ho! ye who wait where sleeps in state
The silent form of SIXTY-EIGHT,
Where from the shadows blue and far
Has come his glinting taper-star,
Where from the carboned upper dark
The crystal scalings of its arc,
In fitful, hither, thither ways,
Are driven like the drifting days,—
Now o'er the winter fields and fells
Ye hear the sobbing Midnight Bells.

Ho! ye whose tears were shed on biers
Of other gray and gathered years,
Why weep ye now, and watch, and wait,
Beside the corse of SIXTY-EIGHT?
The widowed hills, the orphan vales,
May give their anthems and their wails;
May wear their garb of mourning white
Along the pathways of the night,—
But YE! why heed ye now the knells?
Why hearken still the Midnight Bells?

The sunlight smiles through airy miles
On fair and flowered summer isles,
And earth in green and living things,
So gladdened with its lightsome wings,
Floats wanton where the odor-breeze
Goes out the shining summer seas;
But winter from her secret caves
Creeps darkling o'er the ocean waves,
And sad and far from o'er the swells
The bloom has heard its Midnight Bells.

O men who know how sure and slow
The tides of time must ebb and flow;
How one by one the waves must reach
And bear their tribute from the beach,
How sure the sands upon the lea
Go outward to the central sea,
And buried are in hollow grooves
Where slow th' eternal current moves,—
Why pause they where the sounding shells
Bear echoes from the Midnight Bells?

The nations rise, and through the skies
The clamor of their glory flies;
Their flaunting pennons out the gales
Go with the sunlight and the sails,
And spicy isles and frozen zones
Their splendor and their power owns;
But deathless Time — eternal TIME!
He heeds no king, he knows no clime;

And over wars, their shouts, their yells,
He peals the nations' Midnight Bells.

The great, the grand, who gave the land
Their crimson for its right to stand;
Who on their swords of valor brought
Our right of action and of thought;
Who piled their way from kings and thrones
With such a hecatomb of bones,—
Their hearts are still, their forms are cold,
Their very deeds beneath the mold,
And scarce the country's record tells
How we have heard their Midnight Bells.

When tyrant knaves make freemen slaves,
And tread the sod of sacred graves;
When in the darkness and the dust
They give our sabres to the rust;
When in our cells no sound remains
Above the voices of the chains;
When all but memory is dead,
And TIME alone hath ceaseless tread,—
Oh, joy to know a chain foretells
The clanking of their Midnight Bells!

For men whose souls amid the shoals
Are fearless in the tidal rolls;
Who move with shackles on their arms
As proudly in the face of storms

As they whose ermine drapes the gates
Of conquered Empires, fallen States,—
To them shall come no craven gloom,
No haunting shadow of the tomb,
No fear of death, no shrieking hells,
When Freedom swings her Midnight Bells.

The fairest stream that like a dream
Goes down the land, a silver seam;
The stars that show their golden glow
On things that slumber here below;
The waves, the sea, the earth, the sky,
All things that live and all that die;
The great, the good, the weak, the strong,—
To TIME ETERNAL all belong,
And soon or late must come their knells
From sad and solemn Midnight Bells.

In virtue's way to endless day,
Beyond the margin's reaching gray,
Beyond the ether's thick'ning spread,
Beyond the world, beyond the dead,—
Let men, let nations cast their eyes
·Toward the opening Paradise,
Till all the hopes and all the fears,
Till all the chains and all the wars
Are lost forever in the swells
When Heaven tolls our Midnight Bells.

AFTER THE WAR.

WE have filled with recollections
  All our calumets to-day,
And from this clearer present
  Floats the cloudy past away.

We have burned to finer ashes
  All the *débris* of the years,
That so late amid the home-lands
  Brought us misery and tears.

Farewell to all the memories
  That preyed upon our souls,
That made us in our carnage-time
  A populace of ghouls.

Farewell to every record-mark
  Of cruelties and crimes,
And a welcome to the sunlight
  Of dawning better times.

Already from the havoc-fields
  Where rolled the battle-drums,
The busy beat of hammers
  And the din of labor comes;

The plowshare in the sodden ground
  Its fruitful passage takes,
And toil is in its triumph
  From the bayous to the lakes.

O blessed land! where swords are drawn
  To hew the armied grain,
Where lines of corn are stricken down
  Upon the harvest plain;

Where every stalk beneath the stroke
  In golden beauty bows,
And men are counted noble
  Who have sweat upon their brows.

O blessed land! O land of toil,
  And land of human love,
There are pages of repentance
  In thy records up above;

And onward, onward through the days
  Of glory yet to come
Shall march thy legion labor,
  Shall beat their anvil-drum.

Our sinews strong from North to South
  Are wrought of iron bands,
And rivers wind like silver threads
  Adown our shining sands.

Brave Progress with her certain pulse,
  Her mighty breath of steam,
Goes out in power on the earth,
  In glory on the stream.

And Westward far, by plains a-bloom
  And mountains rich in ore,
Our engines bear their burthens
  To the great Pacific shore.

Our sails are white on all the seas,
  With gleaming tracks behind —
At peace to-day with all the world!
  Good-will to all mankind!

Thus much for all the nation
  As a grand majestic whole,
Made up of smaller portions
  As our acts make up the soul.

God hath trusted us with talents,
  Each and all of us a trust;
Howsoe'er we please to use them,
  He is merciful and just.

Let us do our share of labor,
  Let us toil and sweat to-day,
Let us lift our burthened neighbor
  From his falling by the way.

Every impulse of our kindness,
  Every act we do of love,
Hath its record to our credit
  In the archives up above.

*   *   *   *   *   *

By the broad and fair Ohio,
  In the rich lands of the West,
We have builded up our mansions,
  Here to live and here to rest;

And the long grass waves in greenness
  Over plains and over hills,
And the sunlight gives its shimmer
  To the ever-going rills.

Land of Peace and land of Plenty!
  Richer far than any yet:
May thy rising sun of glory
  In the shadow never set!

Goodly arms and sturdy spirits
  Over all thy fields be spread;
Teach the children of thy people
  To be proud to earn their bread!

J

Never plowman trod the furrow
　　Of a richer soil than ours,
To a bosom more prolific
　　Never came the summer showers;

Corn and wheat in rolling billows
　　Flood the acres with their gold,
And the strata spreading under
　　Have a hidden wealth untold.

Build the lordly track of iron
　　Through the pasture-lands and fields,
That its greater strength may gather in
　　And garner up the yields;

Let the palpitating engines
　　Spread their steam adown the valleys,
And the woodlands hanging over
　　Keep its echo in their alleys.

Send the golden harvest outward,
　　Bear away the corn and kine;
Open up the secret treasure
　　Of the underlying mine;

Show the world your share of riches,
　　Give to commerce what you can;
Show the dignity of labor
　　And the worthiness of man!

SIXTY–FIVE

IF a nation hath not goodness then it never can be
    great,
For there's nothing like to virtue in the building of
    a State.
Though you bring your quarried marble from a mul-
    titude of miles,
And rear it into palaces and monumental piles ;
Though with dome and arch and column you may
    beautify the land,
Making earth and air and water pliant agents in your
    hand,
Still without the seal of virtue on the charter of your
    State,
In the eyes of Christian people you are neither good
    nor great ;
In the eyes of God Almighty you are only great in
    sin,
And he'll weigh you in the autumn when His Angel
    garners in.

Let us look a moment calmly o'er the little season
    gone;
Let us mark the boggy places in the road we journey
    on:
There are others to come after in the path which we ·
    have trod,
Let us point them from the quicksand to the way
    upon the sod.

There were mighty throes upon us when we ushered
    in the year
Which yesterday in solemn shroud we saw upon its
    bier;
There were throes as if a giant on our being bent a
    knee,
Admonishing of what we were and what we sought
    to be;
We had coffers heavy laden, we had ships upon the
    brine,
We had fallow-lands and vineyards with their effer-
    vescing wine;
We were strong and stern and haughty from the
    growth of years before,
And our plenitude of glory only made us crave the
    more:
Not such glory as the Christian, in the presence of
    his God,
Hath to come upon his spirit when he bows to kiss
    the rod;
But the vanity of power and the strength of human
    pride,

That had made us scorn the virtues and the honors
    as they died :
So a hand was laid upon us, and our glory stripped
    away
As one might strip a flower-stem upon an autumn
    day.

We have conquered many battles, we have gained a
    world-renown,
We have driven gallant armies and have shaken cities
    down ;
We have laid a land in ashes, we have made a people
    slaves,
We have carried golden trophies from a citadel of
    graves ;
There's blood upon our bayonets and blood upon
    our guns,
And some of it's our brothers' blood and some of
    it's our sons'.
"What boots it how we triumphed so a victory was
    gained !
Who wears the whiter garment may expect to have
    it stained ! "
Thus spoke we in our vanity, our ecstasy of pride,
As one who goes rejoicing o'er the grave of one that
    died ;
So climbed we up the pathway to the pinnacle of
    sin,
And o'er the gulf of darkness we were calmly look-
    ing in.

But the wrath of God was on us, and we felt His
mighty hand
As he stripped the mad ambition of its garments in
the land.
We were "proud and strong and haughty," but within
a little day
We have seen our gilded treasures fast as bubbles
float away:
We are wrecked in pride and fortune; we were rich,
and we are poor;
There's a coffin in our dwelling and a sexton at our
door.

Let us turn the crimson pages in the record-book of
war:
There are giant sins upon us, giant crimes to answer
for:
There are cities laid in ashes, there are desolated
farms;
There are starving children crying in their helpless
mother's arms;
There are widows, there are orphans, cold and home-
less in the land,
With the husband and the father lying fleshless on
the sand;
There is woe and want and sorrow over all the Southern States;
From within the nation's chamber, we can hear it at
the gates;
Yet our flags are flaunting bravely, and our music
fills the air,

For the burthen of the sorrow it is not for us to
    bear ;
We have prison-cells and dungeons thickly peopled
    with the foe,
And some have on the gibbet died, and some are
    dying slow.

Such a fever and such passion over all the North
    has swept,
That though weeping MERCY pleaded, it hath never
    known she wept ;
And the vengeful cry for slaughter from the Puri-
    tanic crowd,
In the halls of central power hath an echo fierce
    and loud ;
From the Northern press and pulpit, from the bench
    and from the bar,
Cometh all the evil pleading of a fury after war.
And but a little while it seems, when frenzy ran so
    high
The nation by a gallows stood to see a woman die—
A woman weak and trembling and as guiltless as a
    child,
But a victim to the fury of a passion fierce and wild.
And here the high offended God put forth His hand
    again,
To write upon the nation's brow the burning mark
    of CAIN.
Again for WIRZ, the foreigner, a wretched feeble man,
But yesterday we filled his cup until it over-ran ;

And one by one we lessen them, these victims to our
    hate,
And there's a thirst for human blood an ocean can
    not sate.

At our helm we had a despot, and for him this crim-
    son tide,
A Nero who could revel while his better subjects
    died ;
But the Mighty Hand o'ertook him in his revel and
    his wrong,
And it taught us in our weakness that the Deity
    was strong.
There are those who call him martyr, there are those
    who call him great :
After *passion* cometh *reason* — let the better spirits
    wait;
As the water finds its level, so the characters of men—
Some may die and be forgotten, some may die and
    live again.
There's a gray-haired man in prison, under iron bolt
    and bar,
A relic and a trophy from the desolating war ;
He was once a mighty leader, such as few are born
    to be ;
He had armies in the nation, he had ships upon the
    sea ;
But our strength in war was greater, for we crushed
    him with our might,
And we watched his day of glory as it settled into
    night.

Now we hold him bound and shackled, with a palsy
    in his arm ;
We have seized and sacked his temple, he is power-
    less for harm.
But to crush and break his spirit, and to take away
    his all,
For the crime of Revolution was a punishment too
    small ;
And the nation must have vengeance, for her women
    cry for blood—
Though it runs a mighty torrent they would have it
    run a flood.
God forgive them all their passion ! God forgive them
    all their sin !
From their hearts drive out the anger, and invoke the
    mercy in !

There's another cry of sorrow from the liberated
    black ;
There is want among his children, and blood upon
    his track.
From his proper grade and level they have thought
    to lift him up,
And he glories at their banquet with a poison in his
    cup. .
From his love and from his labor they have taken
    him away,
And the gloomy night is crowding over all his sunny
    day.
We can hear him in the darkness giving out his bit-
    ter moan,

While for all the bread he asketh they have only
    found a *stone*.
Let him freeze and let him hunger—they are blind
    and cannot see;
It is food and cloth and shelter, and a glory to be
    FREE.
O ye great and godly Christians! O ye Puritanic
    souls,
Have ye lost your human spirits? are ye demons?
    are ye ghouls?
Was it not enough to wreck him in his hopes and in
    his all,
That ye triumph so and revel at his miserable fall?

Though the sins of all the nation in their multitude
    are great,
There are crimes as black and cruel in the records
    of our State;
For Kentucky (God forgive her), though she sought
    to do the best,
From the black and base attrition grew as callous
    as the rest.
There were those who did her murder in the guise
    of right and law;
There's the blood of HUNT upon her, and of CORBIN
    and McGRAW;
And there's such a cry of sorrow from the grave of
    bleeding LONG,
As should pale the cheek of hatred in its memory of
    the wrong.

     *   *   *   *   *   *

God forgive us all our errors! God forgive us all our
    crimes!

We have lived in sin and darkness — let us hope for
    better times.

TO MASTER GEO. W. JOHNSTON.

In youth, my boy, I pray you keep
   This simple truth in view:
That men are only counted great
   For goodly things they do.

The man who lives an aimless life,
   Nor labors every day,
Belongs to that ephemera
   That passes soon away;

But he who takes the labor-tools
   And seeks the science-fields,
Will find the noble harvest that
   The golden autumn yields.

The way to fame is over-grown
   With tangled weeds and vines,
And many take the trodden path
   That from the goal inclines;

But you, my boy, with compass true,
  Must keep the bearing straight,
And cut the stubborn obstacles
  That lie before the gate.

Be guided by the honor-laws
  That gave your kindred name,
And keep the course that ushered them
  Within the walls of fame ;

And when at last the honor-roll
  Above the world is spread,
You will not blush to find your name
  Is written at the head.

HIS LAST· DAY.

As one who from his native place
   In tender youth had turned,
To feel the brown upon his face
   By distant solstice burned;
Who, journey-worn and scarred and sore,
   And sickened with the past,
Has reached again his father's door,
   And tottered in at last;

As one whose memory at home
   Is slowly fading out,
Whose features to his kindred come
   In mistiness and doubt;
Who from the sea has turned again
   The ingle-side to share,
And fled the haunts of stranger men
   To be a stranger *there*.

So I, to-night, a loiterer
   In other paths and lands,

From struggle-scenes and wreck and fear,
   And. *death* upon the sands,
Have turned again an eager gaze
   Upon the homeward track,
And through the mist and through the maze
   Have slowly travelled back.

Here home at last! ah, HOME no more!
   For time hath. hurtled through,
And faces that I study o'er,
   Alas! are strange and new;
All new! all strange, save only one,
   The old Familiar there;
And Time his silver-work hath done
   Upon the master's hair.

I keep the outline of his face
   As faithfully of late,
As when with early artist-grace
   I "did him" on the slate:
The kindly eye, the open brow,
   The lips that ever smiled, ·
I mark them just as truly now
   As when I was a child.

The bold front teeth, the queer-turned nose
   (Your pardon, sir, I pray),
The forward step upon the toes,
   They seem like yesterday.

Though Time hath fled with gray and brown,
  I mark him just as well
As when he pulled the old rope down
  And tied me to the bell.

Full thirty years have fleeted by
  Since first the school began,
And from a little urchin I
  Have grown to be a man;
But I would dash the cares of men .
  And give — I cannot tell —
If he could take me back again
  And tie me to the bell.

The dear companions of my class,
  Habitués at play,
Have some of them gone down the glass,
  And some live *great* to-day.
I've watched the progress of them all,
  And in the ways of fame
I hear at every honor-call
  Some well-remembered name.

The pulpit and the bench and bar,
  The science-fields of earth,
The blood-red annals of the war
  Are vocal with their worth.
Throughout the land, from East to West,
  From Erie to the Keys,
The spirits known and loved the best
  Were nurtured here — like these.

When late, for sad fraternal strife
  Our battle lines were drawn,
And North and South alike were rife
  With armies marching on,
A portion of the early class
  On either side were found ;
And some are 'neath the trampled grass,
  And some live yet renowned.

All honor to the dust of those   .
  Who in the struggle fell,
Who grew as friends but met as foes,
  And fought each other well ;
Their soldier-graves shall long attest
  To future passers-by,
That *dulce et decorum est*
  Pro patria mori.

I come to-night with weary heart
  And saddened eye, to find
Some vestige of the scholar-art
  Left years ago behind :
The labors of the early age,
  The mysteries of school,
The art to scan a Virgil page,
  The Algebraic rule.

From other scenes and other toils
  Too late, alas ! I turn ;
      K *

The science-lamps their sacred oils
   No more for me shall burn.
The springs of youth that joyous sped
   Their courses to the river,
Have mingled with the waves, and fled
   The flower-ways forever.

What though a stranger in the throng
   That now the master sways,
I claim the right to give my song
   The flush of other days ;
And here upon this honored stand
   A gratitude to show
To him who gave a guiding hand,
   So many years ago. .

Ah, more than all, to-night should band
   The early friends and true,
To take the master's honest hand,
   And bid him here adieu ;
Nay, let the gush of tender years
   Adown their channels run ;
The labor of his thirty years
   Is well and nobly done.

ELMWOOD.

I, ALONE of all at Elmwood —
  I, alone of all,
Hear the night-sands dropping slowly,
  Hear them as they fall.
Over me the spirit's slumber
  That these moments bring,
Has not cast the sombre shadow
  Of the night's narcotic wing.

Wakeful now, and full of feeling
  As the stars of light,
I can count the even-pulses
  Beating through the night;
I can count the palpitations
  Of the vision-driven hearts,
By the great magnetic power
  Which poetic night imparts.

There is one of all at Elmwood,
  One alone of all,

Who would start to know her pulses
　　Echoed up the hall —
Echoed up the gloomy stairway
　　And along the quiet hall —
One who in the glaring day-time
　　Never beats a pulse at all.

Oh I read her, now she sleepeth ;
　　Feast upon her dream ;
Catch the *real* of her spirit
　　In its glory-beam.

We are strangers at the noontide ;
　　She a study deep to me,
She a language dead, a scripture
　　Upon tablets in the sea.
But I read her now at midnight —
　　Read her very soul ;
Oh, I creep upon her slumber
　　Silent as a ghoul ;
And I feast upon her vision —
　　Feast upon it, at the price
Which gave Adam wondrous knowledge,
　　Whilst it lost him — Paradise !

RESPONSE—IMPROMPTU.

I do not forget you — I never have thought
 A moment to check the sweet flow of our love;
I cannot forget what so lately you taught,
 I cannot throw down the bright wreath that you
  wove.

Oh the young bird of Hope, with its plumage of truth,
 That flits in the noontide of life's early spring,
Hath a season so brief in the gardens of youth
 That flowers but once feel the rush of its wing.

Not so when the sun has passed over the hill,
 To the autumn of life with its yellower sheaves;
If Hope comes at all, Oh its melodies fill
 In the long afternoon all the murmuring leaves.

I do not forget you — no, no! while my heart
 Hath been touched with the shadow of seasons
  gone by,

While lamp after lamp hath gone out at the start,
  I cannot believe that all passions will die.

I pray you forego every thought that would give
  But a color of falsehood to what I have said ;
'Twere shame that a spirit so faithless should live —
  'Twere better a friendship so hollow were dead.

Then let us strike hands in that honester way
  That tells to ourselves we are unriven friends ;
So when life shall have come to its twilight and
      gray,
  We may smile at the silvery thread that it sends.

THE DEAD THAT SHONE.

[Read before the Confederate Memorial Association at the decoration of Confederate graves, Maysville, Ky., June 12th, 1883.]

FROM hills that rise with crowning woods
   In light and air a-quiver,
Still send the springs their mimic floods,
   Free tribute, to the river:
From freighted leaves that zephyrs turn
   When morning bends them over,
Still fall the dew-drops on the burn
   That glitters through the clover.

Where shadows rest, where sunbeams play,
   In laughter and in revel,
Still go the brooks a vagrant way
   Toward the lower level.
Through summer green, through autumn brown,
   With steady placid motion,
Still sweeps the blue Ohio down
   To meet the waiting ocean.

Thus is it with all human kind—
  Thus will it be forever!
Man's passage here is well defined
  In rill, and brook, and river;
He cometh as a drop of dew.
  His light a moment showing,
A breath—and fallen, lost to view
  Upon the under-flowing.

This common course, this common end,
  Is true, alas! to nature,
So goes the foe, so goes the friend,
  And every living creature;
And drops make up the little rill,
  The rills make up the river,
They speed to where is lying still
  The ocean wide—Forever!

Who, in some morning's moment brief,
  Hath not been blest and christened,
By dew, that on some flower leaf
  That single moment glistened?
Who hath not seen the rainbow hue,
  When morn is moisture-freighted,
That makes a perfect drop of dew
  The fairest thing created?

What atom in this atom world
  Of ash, and spark and ember,

Is more in human eyes impearled
   Or sweeter to remember?
And who, that through his morning rife
   Shook down the gems in showers,
Hath not, from crowding eve of life,
   Called back the dewy hours.

Some lives flow out from hidden springs
   And are not clearly singled,
They move, a mass of living things,
   Of bodies dark, commingled;
But some are born like drops of dew
   By rainbow arches bounded,
With surface bright and outline true,
   Completely made and rounded.

In memory of such as these
   Who glorified the hours,
We gather here, beneath the trees,
   With knots and wreathes of flowers.
Here, finding peace and perfect rest
   From rill and river motion,
A few that lived and shone the best
   Have found, at last, the Ocean.

And here are typified the dews
   That come, the world adorning,
For these were men of rainbow hues
   Brushed down in life's fresh morning,
L

What matter if they came to sight
   From gowans of the meadow !
They only shone with stronger light
   By reason of the shadow.

But here were some from daisy bloom,
   And here were some from roses ;
On common level in the tomb
   Humanity reposes.
In earth the evil and the just,
   The high and low are blended ;
It's ash to ash and dust to dust
   When human life is ended.

With garlands green and flowers fair,
   ·We come to deck the places,
Where rest the few of virtue rare
   That higher manhood graces.
Upon these mounds that, sprinkled here,
   Disclose the sadder story,
Let living bloom to-day appear
   A semblance frail of glory.

Here lies the dust of men who fell—
   The blood of heroes freeing—
Who nobly gave to principle
   The tribute of their being ;
And some were in the gray of morn
   And some the blue of even,

The older grown, the later born,
   To pride and purpose given.

In Shiloh's bloody battle tide
   By flaming cannon lighted,
When Albert Sidney Johnston died
   A country's hope was blighted.
A monument shall bear his name
   Enduring as the river,
And all of glory, all of fame
   Shall be for him forever.

And humbler names shall take the stone
   And be retained in story—
Let's carve them deep and make them known
   To magnitude of glory ;
For there are heroes yet unsung
   Who lie within the wicket,
"The gallant Pelham "—fearless Young,
   And Lashbrooke, Watts, and Pickett.

From all the wars here rest some dead
   To do the Country honor,
To show what wealth Kentucky shed
   In sacrifice upon her ;
For some there were whose mounds here show—
   Grand actors in the drama—
Who wore the blue in Mexico,
   The gray in Alabama.

God speed the work that keeps in mind
  This grand heroic feature!
That teaches man to love his kind
  And elevates his nature;
That makes him like the drop of dew
  That rests upon the flower,
Of perfect form, of rainbow hue—
  The diamond of his hour.

AT CLEARING.

Two ships weigh anchor in the cove ;
  Two ships slide out the brine ;
And one white-sail is thine, my love,
  And one white sail is mine.

A land of peace, hid in the grey
  Beyond our eyes define !
Will thy ship find its quiet bay,
  Thy ship, my love or mine?

Thou, God, make faith our steering star,
  Through clouds alway to shine,
And bring within Thy harbor-bar
  My wife's white ship and mine.

CURE FOR HEADACHE.

My brain is athrob with a pulsing unrest,
   And fever is over my breath ;
Oh, bury my head in the snow of your breast
   And let me be frozen to death.

UNDERNEATH.

Some tuneful words that in our hearts
  Bisect the prosy courses,
Do, by their rhythm, drive the parts
  Insensibly to verses.

While sadder things the autumn days
  Our outer lives are bringing,
A thousand summer roundelays
  The inner voice is singing.

What though we move in sober coats
  The Quaker masses after?
There's something welling in our throats,
  Unorthodox as laughter.

We take the sacerdotal stole
  And priestly surplice o'er us,

To hide the real music-soul
  And smother down its chorus.

What foolish arts beset us all !
  How we ourselves are tasking !
There's every day a funeral,
  And all the mourners masking.

SIXTY–SIX.

THERE'S a sculptor for the marbles
  Over all the buried years,
And his smooth and polished labor
  In a line of white appears.

He hath cunning with the chisel,
  And hath graved the record in,
Telling what the years departed
  In their living-time have been.

He has now a greater labor,
  Worthy all his better skill;
He has carved us many virtues —
  Let him carve us now the ILL.

From the black Egyptian marble
  Let him build a column high,
That the coming years may mark it
  In their quiet passage by.

Never yet hath sculptor graven
   More of crime or more of sin,
Than is better now for speaking
   What this latter year hath been!

———

We are moving slowly onward
   Through a vista-way of years;
We are looking to a future
   Full of sorrow and of tears;

There is not a light to guide us,
   Not a gleam upon the sky;
All our hopes are dead and buried,
   All our joys have flitted by.

We are not the Christian nation
   That we once were thought to be,
When with common voice we worshipped
   "From the centre to the sea."

We are not a godly people;
   We are very far away
From the path that leadeth outward
   To the everlasting day.

Let us see how much of virtue
   We have left in all the store,
Where a world hath looked and wondered
   In the happy days before.

Let us see how great and godly
  Are the acts of those who take
On themselves the nation's ermine
  For the troubled nation's sake.

First of all, we dare be tyrant—
  We who thought the English sway
Over torn and trampled Erin
  Should be rudely dashed away;

We who wept for bleeding Poland,
  And our Christian flag unfurled,
That its folds might flaunt defiance
  Unto all a tyrant world.

We have learned another lesson
  In the onward march of time,
And we build our greatest virtue
  From the fabric of a crime;

And we spurn aside the maxim
  That "your truer blood will show;"
That "he is most ignoble
  Who would trample on a foe."

*   *   *   *   *   *

We have swept our foreign legions
  Over all the Southern bands—
They were fewer than the Spartans,
  We were many as the sands—

And because of all their courage,
  All their stubbornness in fight, .
All their pride of birth and section,
  All their love of human right,

We must put our feet upon them —
  We must crush and bend them low,
Lest their better blood and breeding
  In the future "come to show."

This is Christian, this is proper,
  This is Puritanic law,
And we see the goodly future
  As our Plymouth fathers saw.

What are *they* that we should love them?
  They are little of our kin;
Seldom yet hath Southern current
  Let the Northern current in.

Proud of blood and proud of bearing,
  Quick in anger to a foe,
Never yet hath given insult
  Been without attendant blow.

We are calmer, better balanced,
  We are cooler in our veins;
We have less of heart in battle,
  More of calculating brains;

We are not a kindred people,
  And the passage yet of years
Will not mix the Plymouth waters
  With the blood of Cavaliers!

Next, we claim a godly power,
  And we widen out our span
When we raise the apish negro
  To the standard of a man.

This we do for godly reasons—
  Such our early fathers gave,
"That the servant may be master,
  And the master may be slave."

Thus we raise him from the level
  To his greatest earthly goal,
And we take away his instinct,
  And we give him back a soul—

Such a soul as we are given,
  Such a soul as makes him great:
He is worthy of the chancel,
  He is worthy of the State!

He may come into our circles,
  He may mingle with our blood,
He shall be our equal brother
  As he was before the Flood.

M

Though the curse of God was on him,
  Though he wandered in the land,
We would give him whitest vesture,
  We would take him by the hand.

In the summer all our meadows
  Were a-bloom with scented hay,
And the corn upon our acres
  Spread its fullness far away;

All the shadows of the woodland
  Were astir with heavy kine,
And the hill-sides gave their treasure
  From the rich Catawba vine.

Far indeed from cold and hunger,
  Far indeed from want and woe,
We are in the golden current,
  In the glory of its flow.

Let the people down below us,
  In the desolated land,
Starve and shiver in the palaces
  They built upon the sand;

We have corn and wine and vesture —
  Let it rot and let it mould;
They have nothing now to give us,
  Neither human love nor gold.

O ye rich and pampered people!
  O ye cold and cruel men!
They have crossed your swords in battle,
  They were one and you were ten!

Dare you press your heel upon them,
  When ye usher back the day
That your full and feasted legions
  Fled before the starving *Grey?*

Are ye cowards, are ye cravens
  That ye fear to let them live?
Can ye see a nation perish
  Whilst ye have the food to give?

They had richer fields and vineyards,
  Better homes and broader lands,
Till ye threw the torch among them
  From your desolating bands.

They were proof against your valor,
  They had better-tempered steel —
Think ye now your servant Hunger
  Will be proud to see them kneel.

Not to you, O callous stranger!
  Not to baser blood and birth
Will the true chivalric Southron
  Bend his knee upon the earth.

Better starve amid the ruins
    Of his fallen arch and dome!
Better die amid the ashes
    Of his violated home!

Not for cold nor not for hunger
    Will he kiss your iron rod:
There's an altar for his kneeling,
    It is only to his God!

What of him who, great and noble,
    Stood so very long at bay,
Whilst the veterans drawn around him
    Left their crimson in the way?

Still in bondage, still in prison,
    Living still yet near to death,
Never yet hath human being
    Drawn on earth a prouder breath

First among his race and kindred,
    First among his noble clan,
He has taught a cruel nation
    How to suffer as a man.

All that cunning, all that malice,
    All that human hate can do,
All that any Christian martyr
    In his dying ever knew,

He has known and felt and suffered,
  And his spirit liveth still,
Something more than mortal courage,
  Something more than human will.

Oh that they could learn to conquer!
  Oh that they could come to know
How the truer way is opened
  To the bosom of a foe!

Not by bars of steel and iron,
  Not by rack and torture here,
Can ye force the higher spirit
  From its great and only sphere.

Throw your prison-gates asunder,
  Strike the iron from his hand,
Bid him walk the earth a freeman,
  Make him equal in the land;

Show him first that you are noble,
  Let him see that you are brave,
Act no longer as a coward,
  Be not brutal as a slave.

While he lingers in the shackles
  He is master of you all,
He is freer than the sentry
  In your very prison-hall;

M *

He is better, prouder, freer
  Than the proudest of your State ;
He can teach you what is noble,
  He can show you what is great.

May the angels at his pillow
  ` Their undying vigils keep !
God preserve his Southern children,
  Who are praying as they weep !

*   *   *   *   *   *

As the fire hid in ashes
  Under mountains of the earth,
When its red volcanic lava
  Struggles into upper birth,

There are words that come unbidden,
  And the lips are burst apart
By a passion leaping upward
  From its covert in the heart.

Though we bury wrongs, to hide them
  From our own and other eyes,
There are those that in us quicken,
  For the spirit never dies ;

And upward from the charnel
  Come the living that were dead,
All the olden wounds upon them,
  All the marks of where they bled.

Oh that crimes and wrongs were fewer !
  Oh that men were better grown !
Oh that veins had less of fever !
  Oh that hearts had less of stone !

*　　*　　*　　*　　*　　*

Brave Kentucky ! brave, but laggard
  When her sisters gave their blood,
She has walked into the current
  With her bosom to the flood ;

She has dared to give example
  To the cruel-hearted States,
When she meets her Southern children
  With a welcome at her gates.

Though a tyrant held her silent
  In the shadow of her guns,
She had all a mother's yearning
  For the glory of her sons ;

And with chains upon her person,
  And a hand upon her mouth,
She had not a pulse within her
  But was beating for the South.

Better far than poor Missouri,
  Better far than Tennessee,
And Virginia, best of any,
  Better now than she.

Ah, Virginia! torn and bleeding,
  O'er the ashes of her dead
Let the tears of queenly woman
  Be the requiem that is said.

Though they build no pallid marble
  O'er the silence of their graves,
There are tombs in fairer bosoms
  For Virginia's fallen braves.

Pass, O seasons, spring and summer!
  Come again, O winter cold!
TIME shall never lose the record,
  TIME shall hear the story told!

Truth has more of spirit-feature,
  Falsehood more of human cast;
Nations yet unborn shall hear it,
  Truth shall conquer at the last.

LEE.

We saw the fragile maiden, May,
  Trip down the paths of morning,
And queen July in central day,
  Her flower-throne adorning;

And weeping trees in sombre lines
  Took up an anthem murmur,
When August, with her trailing vines,
  Went out the gates of Summer.

Now yellow husks are on the grain,
  And leaves are brown and sober,
And sundown clouds have caught again
  The flush of ripe .October;

We hear the woody hill-tops croon,
  The airy maize-blades whisper,
The year is in its afternoon,
  And leaf-bells ring the vesper.

What is it gives this gloaming-song
    Its melancholy feature?
What is it makes our souls prolong
    This monotone of nature?

What tearful grief is in our hearts —
    What swaying under-reason?
What sorrow real now imparts
    Its spirit to the season?

The crisping leaves may shoal the ways,
    The sun turn down the heavens —
Still all the years have fading days,
    And all the days have evens:

Enough — whatever else may be —
    That in this autumn weather,
The verdure of the world and LEE
    Have silent fled together.

So prone are men where'er they move
    To tread the ways of evil,
They seldom hold their kind above
    A common grade and level;

But LEE, beside his fellow-man,
    Stood, over all, a giant —
The higher type — the perfect plan —
    God fearing, God-reliant.

A giant not alone in fields
  Where bent· the sanguine Reaper,
Where Death threw o'er his harvest-yields
  An autumn crimson deeper ;

But with an iron strength of will
  He sought his life to fashion ;
He held his ruder pulses still,
  And closed the gates of passion.

There have been men whose mighty deeds,
  On cold historic pages,
Are driven like October seeds
  Along the reaching ages ;

Whose statues stand like sentinels,
  On whited shafts and bases,
Whose ashes rest in marble cells,
  And sepulchres and vases ;

But he who in this autumn time
  Was lost beyond the river,
Has found a glory-path to climb,
  Forever and forever !

And monumental marble here,
  With deeds of honor graven,
What can it be to one so near
  The inner gates of Heaven?

By still Potomac's margin dun,
  Where shrilly calls the plover,
Where lean the heights of Arlington
  Its glassing waters over,

No autumn voices haunt the moles,
  No breezy covert ripples,
No longer whirl the leaves in shoals
  Beneath the stately maples ;

Some vandal's axe has shorn the crest,
  The woody slopes are shaven, .
No longer builds the dove her nest
  Where mournful croaks the raven ;

But down the Southland's fruity plain
  The leaves are all a-quiver,
And *there* his memory shall reign
  Forever and forever !

THE DEVIL'S HOLLOW.

On Devil's hill
The Day-king still
His amber robe is trailing;
Floats up to sight
The Queen of night,
Her white, sweet face unvailing.
In silver cars
The courtier stars
With leal allegiance follow;
As kling-go-ling
The cow-bells ring
From out the Devil's hollow.

How smooth and hard
The boulevard
This autumn eve for walking;

x

Beneath the cliffs,
In misty skiffs,
I hear the fishers talking ;
Above the bridge,
'Round Devil's ridge,
Still flits the tardy swallow,
As kling-go-ling
The cow-bells ring
From out the Devil's hollow.

Oh, mystic scene !
The still ravine !
The bridge ! the elm ! the river !
For love and rhyme
This twilight time
Should linger here forever ;
No meeter field
Was e'er revealed
For Daphne or Apollo,
As kling-go-ling
The cow-bells ring
From out the Devil's hollow.

Though nights to be
Come fair to me,
Beyond my fancy's bringing,
When light shall steer
Some gondolier,
With maids to gittern singing,

From distance long,
Shall float the song,
Above their tra-la la-la,
The klang-go-lang
The cow-bells rang
A-down the Devil's hollow.

THANKSGIVING.

For meet dispense of shine and rain
    On mold and sod ;
For gathered seeds, for garnered grain,
    Give thanks to God !
Give thanks for fecund summer fields ;
Give thanks for fullest autumn yields.

For greening stools of growing wheat
    In spring to nod ;
For present grace, for promise sweet,
    Give thanks to God !
Give thanks for fruity tree and vine ;
Give thanks for raiment, meat, and wine.

For pleasures spread, for riches veined
    Through paths untrod ;

For realms to seek, for realms attained,
    Give thanks to God !
Give thanks for glory pre designed ;
Give thanks for muscle, manhood, mind !

For steerage clear beyond the shoals ;
    .For sparing rod ;
For peace, for hope, for deathless souls,
    Give thanks to God !
Give thanks for life, for action free,
For all that is and is to be !

CHANGE.

PINK-CHEEK'D, blue-eyed, and fair,
With swirls of golden hair
On shoulders bare,
I saw them every-where. '
Upon my round,
I found,
Throughout the street,
Their faces sweet—
Girl-children—little motes
Of womanhood,
With voices in their throats
Like those that fill the wood
When winter breaks
And man awakes
To know that God is good.
Sweet girls,

That went along
With song
And laughter,
Not recking of the after,
But flitting in the sun and shade,
As they were made
Like flowers are,
All fair,
And fresh, and sweet,
Creation to complete.

But yesterday
Upon my way
I saw them, at their ease,
With petticoats above the knees,
Go through the pool,
'A joyous way to school.
It seems so short a time,
It does not chime
With truth to say,
'T was yesterday ;
And, yet,
I almost think their feet are wet,
As now I see them pass—
New pictures in the glass—
Lithe maids,
With gathered braids
And hooded heads,
Young thoroughbreds !
With hair gone up and skirts gone down—

The glory of the town !
They broke the bonds of barefoot play
Since yesterday.

And this is change !
In all the range
Of human sight,
Through shade and light,
It cometh every-where—
The very air
Doth change its temper in the year
The birds of spring appear ;
The grasses grow
And streams are set aflow ;
And while we look
The brook
Is closéd o'er ;
The bud hath blossomed on the shore,
And from a brief
Existence in the leaf,
It turneth down
Unto the grass grown brown.

Some change, upon my round
I note on every ground ;
New features 'wake
As hidden crysalides break,
And all things take
A new complexion in the sun,
As, one by one,
The sure sands run.

The barefoot girl
With straggling curl
And careless swing,
Became another thing
In time ;
She did not climb,
And wade the pool,
Her later maiden way to school :
With modest looks
She bore her books,
And as she passéd,
Nor slow, nor fast,
Went as she should,
The stately way of womanhood !

·So with the boy :
His toy
Is thrown aside ;
He does not ride
With such exultant speed.
The old velocipede.
As days go by
His eye
Hath compassed greater things ;
He swings
A wider circle now.
His brow
Begins to ache for bays
To crown it in his latter days ;
He seeks a plan

To make the man,
And puts away
His yesterday.

And so again,
With men,
They seek a wider range,
And greater change
Of after-life ;
Grow weary of the strife
And moil
And toil
Of earth,
They seek the newer birth—
The peace and quiet of the grave,
And Him who died to save.

This law
Should give us awe.
This never-failing course
Of Nature's force,
Is planned
Upon a basis grand.
The cunning Maker of the scheme
Hath coséd every seam.
And finished every part
With perfect art.

We have our days
Of great amaze,

At all the wonders done
Beneath the sun.
We see
The little seed that makes the tree.
It taketh root,
And beareth leaf, and bud, and fruit ;
And leaf must brown, and fruit must fall,
And death must follow after all.
We note the rain
Shed over hill and plain,
And streams in laughter
Coming after,
Until the land, its yellow blood
Gives up to make the flood ;
And when the cloud has pass'd,
The sun at last,
Comes out to drink the sea ;
The water goeth from the lea,
And, by and by,
The earth is dry,
And newer clay
Is in the field of yesterday.

The days and years,
Alternate, come with smiles and tears,
And *all* this rule of change must keep,
And all must smile, and all must weep.
He smiles the best who weeps the most,
And neither smile nor tear is lost.
The tear is rain—the smile is sun—

We could not part with either one.
In day we wake,
In night we sleep;
In youth we smile,
In age we weep;
And sweet our early childhood seems,
And sweeter still our later dreams,
And sweet, through all the days and years,
Are all our smiles and all our tears;
We take the whirl
Through every grade,
From barefoot girl
To lissom maid—
From maid to woman—youth to man—
And keep, throughout, the perfect plan.

GOOD-NIGHT.

"Wait till the moon goes down—
Wait yet a little time," she said,
And to the trellis leaned her head,
    In braids of autumn-brown.

    Both her still hands in mine,
Full close I stood and caught her sighs,
And looked great love in sweet, wide eyes,
    And made no other sign,

    And westward went the moon,
And brighter grew the craggy edge—
The silver turrets of the ledge
    Must hide its glory soon.

    It was not *soon* to me ;
I felt the moments grown to years,
With my lips on the verge of hers—
    Dead shells beside the sea.

o*

Cold were my lips like shells,
As there I saw the white tulle float,
A misty sea about her throat
    A sea of foamy swells.

And closer still I stood,
And colder grew, and trembled strong,
And then red lava ran along
    The alleys of my blood.

And still her hands, so white,
So small, I held in mine so great,
Until the moon went down in state,
    And then I said " good-night! "

WHEN school "lets out" at sun-down time,
And shadows long up hill-sides climb,
With leap and romp and laugh and shout,
In kilt and smock and roundabout,
By grain-field fence, through pasture-grass,
A foot-worn way, her scholars pass;
And bright-faced elf and brown-faced lout
Go heart-glad home, when school "lets out."

I sit and watch, where, white and slow,
The mistress moves in grace below :
A lithe young girl, with folded hands,
With low-down locks in wide, brown bands,
Who floats in light where deep shade lies,
With sweet, sad looks in lake-blue eyes ;
I sit and watch, and hope and doubt
I know not what, when school "lets out."

171

Were I so young as they who know
The mild maid rule, just there below:
Would I be glad as they who pass
By grain-field fence and pasture-grass?
Would I be glad the home bound way,
And laugh and shout and romp as they?
It might be so in roundabout,
But not, as now, when school " lets out."

Some day—how soon I can not tell,
But some day soon, I know full well—
My feet shall fall with beat as slow
The green-laid way that hers do go,
And I shall feel my great heart rise
To tender looks from lake-blue eyes,
And there shall be no fear, no doubt,
Her hand in mine, when school " lets out."

CHRISTMAS.

The day had gathered from the night,
   When, in God's truth abiding,
There came three men on camels white
   From out the desert riding—
Three heralds gray, that through the morn
   Were speeding fast and faster,
Proclaiming loud: " The King is born!
   We come to serve the Master!"

And days have been, and days have gone,
   And years on years have darkened,
Since in that blessed Christ-day morn,
   The three wise men were hearkened;
And still, through all the maze of years
   That constant Time is summing,
To trustful eyes there yet appears
   Three snow white camels coming.

o*

Oh, let it fall, or clear or gray,
  With sunshine or with shower,
Our Holy Master's natal day
  Shall have no saddened hour.
God send His fairest Christmas morn !
  God free all souls from trammels !
Let men proclaim : " The King is born !"
  Let all see three white camels.

THE BOURBON HORSE-THIEF.

A STILL, fall night in the fields of Bourbon ;
   The dip burnt down in the breeder's room ;
Lamplight faint in the distance urban ;
   Starlight faint in the mist-thick gloom.

Ten by the clock from the spire at Paris ;
   The moon not up, but the east sky gray ;
Knee-deep grass in the grove where the mare is ;
   Wide green meads in the lands away.

Full three score miles to the hills of Rowan ;
   Six full hours till the red daybreak ;
I'll ride as the crow flies—grass and gowan—
   A grand blood-bay, or a grave at stake !

My black mare champs in the locust thicket ;
   A nostril wide and a nicker low ;
A true vedette to a hard-by picket—
   Steady, good girl !—there 's blood to go.

Cope, boy! cope, boy—he's nearing the cover—
  Cope, boy! cope, boy—be steady there, Prue—
He scents the corn and he leaves the clover;
  Gods! what a mount for a grand review!

Ho, boy! so-h boy! ha! curse on his shying!
  A true speed strain, or I know no hoof!
Ho, boy! cope, boy! he's offish; how trying!
  Merciless villain, to stand aloof!

Hither, my girt, come out of the shadow;
  Teach the Adonis there's naught to fear.
A queen of the road! a king of the meadow!
  Death and the devil! the moon is here.

So-h! coming at last! now, beauty, be still!
  A silk-soft flank, a grip at the nose;
There's ever a way for a right good will;
  Saddle and spur, and away he goes.

Follow, my lass; no moment to squander;
  It's forty miles to the mouth of Slate;
Venturesome here, but it's dangerless yonder—
  Beautiful stride as we cleared the gate!

Over the rise, in shade of the maples,
  And down the slope to Stoner's ford.
A risk, mayhap, to run in the ripples—
  A thorough-bred or—a cooling-board.

Good! here we are! no tide in the water!
  Hist! what is that on the other side?

A Paris beau and the breeder's daughter—
  Taking it late for a lover's ride.

Bother the fool ! he stared at the horses ;
  He turned in saddle to see the bay ;
He 'll ride right hard if he rides my courses ;
  The hills of Rowan or Hell by day !

Here, over the wall to the left ; it's better
  By far to lope in the rye just now.
The black mare knows that a midnight clatter
  Is not correct in the road, somehow.

A ten-rail panel ahead.   We 'll throw it ;
  A rail and a rider is all we need.
There, now it 's down ; why, a scrub could go it ·
  It is n't a break for a blooded steed.

Hark ! my ear is at fault, or the air is ;
  What a murmuring noise in the corn ;
There ! it 's back in the region of Paris ;
  And i'ts somebody blowing a horn.

Blow on, poor fool, till your lungs are tested ;
  The trump of a chase is joy to me ;
The bay is fresh, and the black is rested ;
  The moon is up and the fields are free.

Hinkston is here, like a silken ravel,
  Its white line laid on a ground of green.
The wind is slow to the way we travel—
  A hoof unheard and a horse unseen.

Oh! for a war in the world ; · a strider
   Equal to this for a hasty raid !
Glory for two of us—horse and rider—
   Ah ! this is the way that names are made.

Bath already, for yonder is Bethel ;
   It 's just an hour to the mouth of Slate ;
The Fat Creek Knobs and the glens of Athol ;
   The horns of Bourbon were blown too late.

Nothing to fear in the fells of Licking !
   The ford is fair and the water low.
I crossed it once when the ice was breaking—
   It was n't a time to travel slow.

What 's that? only the spit of a rifle.
   Somebody 's tithing a herd to-night.
A fool, to risk so much for a trifle—
   A light below and the town in sight.

People must live, and cries of the younger
   Go never unheard, at night, for food ;
Property laws and the laws of hunger
   Are not the make of a common mood.

Answered ! so ho ! and over the border !
   A signal shot from the other side !
A slacker rein, and the spur in order !
   It 's coming at last—the time to ride.

Off like a bolt, and faster and faster !
   It 's safe if only we pass the town !

Go, my steed, for yourself and your master;
  They 'll have to ride if they ride us down.

Over—hurrah for the hills of Rowan!
  A foam-white flank, but the danger past;
Over the grass, and over the gowan—
  The village of Morehead gained at last;

Two score and a half, and a half to go—
  A merry dash by a mellow moon;
They beat the break in the briars below,
  But bantered the game a bit too soon.

I ride right on to the star of morning!
  A red brush bound to a shaly way!
Was ever a prize so worth the earning—
  Ever such blood as the Bourbon bay!

After us still? a pack of the beagles!
  Treachery here in the uplands free!
Cowardly dogs, in sight of the eagles:
  Better they never be known to me!

Powder again! the sing of a missile!
  They try to rival my run with lead.
I know the piece by the pellet's whistle:
  It isn't the first has grazed my head.

The black mare down! O, murderous devil!
  He hadn't the soul of her he smote!
The day shall come, and he pray and drivel,
  And bleat and beg—my grip at his throat.

Good-bye, good friend! Ah, never a truer
  Under the thigh of a soldier strode.
Thus all drop out: grow fewer and fewer:
  There bleeds my best in the Rowan road.

Speed on, brave boy! the haven is yonder—
  A blue line under a rare red sky:
Give them a roll of your heels in thunder
  Over the beds of the branches dry.

A shot in the leg! no matter, go on!
  A little time and we end the chase:
Farewell, fair night! there is hope in the dawn—
  A sorry road, but a splendid race.

My bridle arm! well, go at your pleasure:
  Volley away, ye vulturing knaves!
Less than a mile at the front to measure,
  The yellow brush and the Yocum caves.

Hit in the back! the gallop is over,
  These are the breaks of the Rowan hills!
It's hard to fall in front of the cover—
  Oh, God! it is n't the shot that kills.

NOTES.

IT was not thought necessary to introduce these poems with any apologetic preface, as no apology ought to excuse an act of this kind; but the author takes advantage of these notes to say that his verses are an accumulation of the rubbish of boyhood and youth, mixed with a few expressions of his later manhood. A demand for such a collection has existed among his friends for several years, and he has taken advantage of terms offered by his publisher to prepare this volume, without a further design than that of gratifying those who have manifested a personal interest in him and his writings.

The poem entitled LEE, was hastily prepared after this book was ready for press. The subject was worthy a far higher tribute than any tongue or pen could offer; but those who know the author will see in the lines a *desire* to do honor to the memory of the great and good man; and what more can be done?

SHE appeared in the *Yeoman*, at Frankfort, Ky., in August last. It was severely handled by a writer in the *Cincinnati Enquirer*, who thought "for the sake of letters," poetry of that sentiment had better not be encouraged. It was evident from the character of the paragraphs, that he who wrote was perhaps as appreciative of the lines as the author himself. The poem, if it may be called

N

such, was never intended for any other purpose than that o
eliciting remark. It succeeded in this particular case, if not n
general.

The poems SIXTY-FIVE and SIXTY-SIX, were written in the
years indicated, and published as New Year addresses. The
apostrophe to Kentucky in the last poem, was occasioned by
the circumstance of the repeal of an Expatriation law by the
Legislature.

The MONEYLESS MAN appeared for the first time in 1855.

The BIVOUAC pictures a condition of the Confederate soldiery
as existing at Bull's Gap, in 1862.

UNDER THE PINES was produced on an outpost near the City
of Richmond, one night in 1864.

The lines entitled HIS LAST DAY, were written upon a few
hours' notice, and read at the closing exercises of Rosemont
Academy. Mr. W. W. Richeson, the tutor, had been in charge
of a school at Maysville, Ky., for thirty-seven years, and this occa-
sion was the last upon which he would officiate there in that
capacity. He had taught the parents and grand-parents of some
of his scholars, and was greatly beloved in the community.

The lines addressed to MASTER GEO. W. JOHNSTON, were
written on his birthday. He was then twelve years of age, and
had already distinguished himself by a long retention of a place
on the "roll of honor" at an excellent school. His development
of character now gives high promise of later worth.

FALLEN was one of the author's early efforts. It was first
published in the *Illustrated News* at Richmond, Va., in 1862, but
had been written several years before.

THE LITTLE BOY GUIDING THE PLOW was written at "Tally's
Church," a small log-house in East Tennessee, in 1864. The
condition of that section at the time was such as the poem
represents.

A lady of Virginia gave the author a NASTURTIUM FLOWER in memory of Swain's conceit —

"A spirit dwel's in every flower."

She said a fairy inhabited the one she gave, which she hoped would inspire a poem. The verses were written in camp that night.

THE FAITH SHE PLIGHTED ME is founded upon an actual circumstance. The unfortunate gentleman, however, still lives, having fairly forgotten his disappointment in the possession of a new love.

www.ingramcontent.com/pod-product-compliance
Lightning Source LLC
Chambersburg PA
CBHW022357020726
47500CB00002B/319